Painting
the Black

Painting
the Black

Carl Deuker

Houghton Mifflin Company
Boston

For information about this and other Houghton Mifflin
trade and reference books and multimedia products, visit
The Bookstore at Houghton Mifflin on the World Wide Web
at http://www.hmco.com/trade/.

The text of this book is set in 11.5 point Janson.

Library of Congress Cataloging-in Publication Data
Deuker, Carl.
Painting the black / by Carl Deuker.
p. cm.
Summary: When star athlete Josh Daniels moves in across
the street, Ryan Ward doesn't realize how much his life will
change during his senior year at Seattle's Crown Hill High.
ISBN 0-395-82848-1
[1. Self-perception — Fiction.   2. Baseball — Fiction.
3. High schools — Fiction.   4. Schools — Fiction.]   I. Title.
PZ7.D493No   1997
[Fic] — dc20   96-23763   CIP   AC

Printed in the United States of America
BP   10   9   8   7   6   5   4   3   2

For Anne, Marian, and Hammy

The author would like to thank Ann Rider,
the editor of this book,
for all the help she has given him.

Part One

▪ 1 ▪

Lots of guys can stand on the pitcher's mound and throw a baseball hard. But they aren't pitchers. A pitcher does more than throw: he knows what he's doing out there. He changes speeds; he works the corners, inside and outside, tying batters up or making them reach out awkwardly. And once he owns the corners, once the umpire is calling all those pitches strikes, then he really goes to work. He moves his pitches out or in another inch, so that instead of going over the plate, the ball passes over the edge of the plate. Painting the black, they call it, putting the ball right there on the borderline. Josh Daniels could do that. He lived on that borderline. I know because I was his catcher.

A year ago I would have sworn that I could never play baseball again, that it was absolutely impossible for me to make the school team. But I was right there with Josh when he reached out for that championship ring. My hand was right next to his. Even now I'm not sure who wanted it more.

3

It all started one night last June. I'd been listening to the Mariners' game. It was one of those three-hour slug-fests that went back and forth. We were down two in the last of the ninth when Ken Griffey Jr. came up with the bases loaded. Griffey took the first pitch low, then he got one in his wheelhouse and blasted it. I was only listening, but I swear I could see that drive, see the ball climbing higher and higher and then landing in the second deck. The radio exploded, and my heart just about came out of my chest.

After a game like that, you can't just turn off the radio and knock off. I listened to the post-game show and the manager's show, but I was still too pumped up to sleep.

I switched to one of those stations that play old rock. I had the sound down low because my mom and dad had been in bed for hours. That's why I picked up the rumble of the engine the moment the truck turned and headed up our block. And when the truck stopped, engine idling, in front of the big empty house across the street, I went over to the window to look out.

The sky was cloudless, with a big full moon overhead. The passenger door opened and a kid who looked to be about my age, seventeen or eighteen, hopped out. I could see him clearly in the moonlight. A big kid with dark, shoulder-length hair and a long, angular face.

The driver, a man I figured was his father, stuck his head out the window. His voice carried in the night air. "I'm going to pull this thing right up to the steps. You guide me, Josh."

The kid climbed onto the porch. He put both hands

up and motioned for the truck to back toward him. "Keep coming. Keep coming." His rich, deep voice filled the night air. "A little more . . . easy now . . . stop!" The brake lights went on, and for an instant his face turned an eerie red, making him look like a rock star in some MTV video.

The driver's door opened and the man, who was short and stocky, stepped out. "Give me the house keys," he said, looking back into the truck.

A woman's voice answered from inside. "I don't have them. You've got them."

"I do *not* have them." The man's voice was sharp.

A search took place, the keys were found, and the front door to the house opened. The porch light went on, the rolling back door of the truck was raised, and the unloading began.

If it had been daytime, I would never have stood at that open window and watched, and not just because they could have seen me. Time passes differently late at night. You can stand and look out a window without worrying that you should be doing something else. Those late hours are all stolen hours.

They didn't unload all that much. Mattresses, box springs, some lamps, a table — just the basics. There was probably some other stuff too, but I didn't pay much attention. Mainly I watched the kid, the way he took the stairs three at a time, his broad shoulders, his rail-straight back.

When I was in sixth grade, I broke my ankle and had to spend a couple of weeks in the hospital. Day after day

I'd lie in bed and watch "Leave It to Beaver" reruns on the hospital television. All the time I watched, something seemed strange about the program, but I could never quite put my finger on it. Just before I got out of the hospital, I figured out what it was: Every time Beaver stepped outside, someone his age was there waiting to do something with him. Kids lived in every house up and down Beaver's block.

I don't know about the rest of this country. Maybe it's still that way in some places. But in the Crown Hill neighborhood of Seattle where I live, there are old people, young couples with no kids, and single people. I've lived in this same house my whole life. In all that time, there had been only one year when anybody my age lived on this block — and that year ended in disaster. So seeing somebody my age was something different.

They worked for about an hour. Then the front door closed and the porch light went off. I found myself yawning, so I went back to my bed. I listened to a couple more songs on the radio. The last one I remember was "Hey Jude." Somewhere in one of those *Na Na Na Na*'s at the end, I fell asleep.

▪ 2 ▪

It was nine when I woke up the next morning. I heard my mom grinding coffee downstairs in the kitchen. The lawn mower was going in the front yard. Early to bed and early to rise — that's my parents.

I was about to roll over and go back to sleep when I remembered the truck and the face in the moonlight. I went to my window and looked out, half-expecting the old green house across the street to be empty and quiet.

But it wasn't. A Ryder truck was parked in the driveway. Boxes were piled up on the front porch. The screen door was propped open and music was coming from an upstairs window.

I had a sudden urge to rush downstairs and across the street. Then I shook my head and laughed at myself. I was acting as if this guy was going to be my best friend for life, when I didn't know the first thing about him. I'd only seen him in the night. He could have been twenty-five years old for all I knew. Or fourteen. Or a complete jerk.

So I did everything the way I normally did: I dressed, I listened to the radio. Boeing had sold some 777's to China. Griffey led the All-Star balloting. It was going to be seventy-one degrees.

I walked to the bathroom, splashed some water on my face, and gave my teeth a quick brushing and my hair a quick combing before heading downstairs. My mother, who sells real estate, was drinking coffee at the kitchen table, the *Seattle Times* spread out in front of her. She was immaculate, as usual. Not a hair out of place, not a wrinkle in her clothes.

"You want bacon and eggs, Ryan?" she asked, looking up. "I'll make some for you."

That was like her too. She hates bacon, hates the

grease that splatters on the stovetop, hates the smell of it in the house. She'd never cook it for herself or for my dad, but she'd cook it for me.

I shook my head. "No, I'll just have some cereal and toast."

I filled a bowl with Cheerios. Then I stuck a couple of slices of rye bread in the toaster and pulled down the knob.

Everything the way I usually did it.

"We've got new neighbors," my mother said as I started on my cereal.

"I know," I answered, feeling a little surge of excitement in spite of myself. "I heard them moving in."

My mother frowned. "I don't doubt it. All of Seattle heard them move in."

I smiled to myself. For the four months the old green house had stood empty, she'd worried that our new neighbors would be noisy.

"How can you be quiet moving in?" I said, teasing her.

"Oh, you can be quieter than they were. And why did they have to move in at midnight? That's what I'd like to know. Criminals move in at midnight."

I shoveled in a mouthful of Cheerios. "Criminals move *out* at midnight."

She snorted, then went back to her coffee and newspaper.

The back door opened and my dad came in. He's going bald, and I could see glistening drops of sweat on the top of his head.

"I need a drink of water," he said, wiping his brow.

If I get hot and sweaty outside, I just take a slug of

water straight from the hose. Not my dad. He's a banker, and he likes everything just so. He got a glass down from the cabinet and filled it from a pitcher of cold water he keeps in the refrigerator from May to October. His first name is Charles, and I've never heard anyone — not even my mom — call him *Charlie* or *Chuck.*

When he finished drinking, he put the glass in the sink and turned to me. "Both lawns are mowed, Ryan. I'd like you to edge them."

"I will," I said. "This afternoon."

"Why not get it done now? It's only going to get hotter."

I finished my toast, then wiped my mouth and stood. "I want to go over and meet our new neighbors."

My mother put down her newspaper. "Why so friendly?"

I shrugged. "I thought I saw a kid about my age last night. I'm going to meet him sometime. It might as well be now."

She straightened in her chair. "I'm not sure that's wise, Ryan. We know nothing about these people. I don't want —"

I felt my teeth clench tight. "Mother," I snapped, "I'm just going to say hello. I'm not going to go into his room and shoot heroin."

"Don't be smart with me, young man. I'm just trying to —"

"Caroline," my father cut her off this time, his voice softer than mine. "Ryan is just going to say hello. That's all."

She looked at him and then at me. "I'm sorry," she said. "I'm being silly. Go and introduce yourself." She reached over and patted my hand. "It's hard for me to realize how grown up you are."

I was angry, and her little pat made me even angrier. I was about to lash out, but I caught my father's eye, and I bit back the words.

I went upstairs to my room, and as I yanked my shoes on and started lacing them up, my anger slipped away. In its place came guilt.

I don't know why I always end up feeling guilty when we have one of those arguments. It's not like I'm responsible for the way I was born. If anyone should feel guilty, it's my dad. The camping trip was his idea.

The whole thing had happened this way: My mom was six months pregnant with me. She'd had a tough time of it. She had thrown up for three months. When that stopped her legs got all swollen, and then she had shooting pains in her back.

My dad has always been a big outdoorsman. Hiking, cross-country skiing, rock climbing — that's what he loves. So when she felt better for a few weeks, he talked her into a camping trip at Crescent Lake on the Olympic Peninsula. That's across the Puget Sound from Seattle, three hours by car and ferry. He said it would be their last chance to get off on their own. She must have wanted to go too, because she's not shy about saying no. She says no to me all the time.

Anyway, the second night out the batteries to their flashlight went dead. My dad was building a fire to barbecue the trout he'd caught, so it was my mom who went to pick up new ones at a little store along the highway.

It was raining hard. My mom had driven a couple of miles when a deer ran onto the road, looked into the headlights, and froze. She slammed on the brakes, skidded, but still hit the deer. It flew onto the hood of the car and crashed through the windshield. Her car skidded off the road.

A trucker came along. He spotted her car in the ditch and the deer's body on the hood. He pulled his logging rig over, raced back, and pried open the front door. My mother was unconscious.

The trucker radioed the State Police; they called for an emergency medical helicopter; and soon she was whirring over the Puget Sound to Children's Hospital in Seattle.

I was born in that helicopter. Two minutes into my life, I stopped breathing. As the chopper was landing on the roof of the hospital, a medic was giving me CPR to bring me back from the dead.

Two pounds nine ounces. That's what I weighed. A real heavyweight. I couldn't breathe right; I couldn't suck right. Twenty years earlier I wouldn't have lived two hours. As it was, I spent my first three months in the hospital.

And it didn't end then. As a little kid I was always sick, always up crying at night, always at the doctor's office with ear and throat infections.

I was ten when I overheard my mom tell my Grandpa Kevin that she couldn't have any more children. I don't know why she couldn't. I didn't know the questions to ask then, and I'd be too embarrassed to ask them now. But I do know it has to do with the way I was born.

Once I'd finished lacing up my shoes that morning, I went back down to the kitchen and gave her a kiss on the top of her head. "What's that for?" she said, looking up.

"Nothing," I answered, and then I was out the door.

▪ 3 ▪

My new neighbor was sitting cross-legged on his porch, a bottle of water next to him. As I crossed the street, I waved to him. Then I pointed my thumb in the direction of my house. "My name is Ryan Ward. I live right across from you."

He stood, and came down the steps toward me, a smile on his face. "I'm Josh," he said, "Josh Daniels." He was even bigger than I'd thought, around six four and at least two hundred pounds. As we shook I was struck by the size and strength of his hand.

We stood there for an awkward twenty seconds or so. "I'm not doing anything today," I finally said. "If you want, I'll give you a hand moving in."

He looked at the boxes on the porch, and then at all the other boxes crowded in the truck. "To tell the truth, I need a break." He paused. "You play baseball? 'Cause if you do, I've got all my stuff in that box right there. If there's a park around here we could play a little catch."

His question was so unexpected it took me a while to answer. "The Community Center is just a couple of blocks away," I finally managed.

He rummaged through the box, pulling out a catcher's mitt, a glove, and a baseball. "Let's get going before my father comes out and puts me back to work."

As we walked down to the Community Center, he asked me if I was still in high school. "I'll be a senior," I answered. "How about you?"

"The same. What's the school like?"

"Crown Hill High? It's okay, but I can't wait to get out."

He nodded. "I know what you mean. High school gets old, doesn't it?"

When we reached the Community Center, his eyes widened. "Everything is so green," he said. "And the grass is so thick. We moved up here from San Jose, and the fields there have been brown for a month."

I laughed. "We do get a little rain up here, you know."

He gave me the catcher's mitt. It was pretty beat-up, but we weren't throwing the ball hard, so that didn't matter. "You play on a baseball team?" he asked.

"I played in grade school. Center field. Then I broke my ankle, and it didn't heal right. Now I can't run well enough to play."

"That's too bad. You must have been fast to play center field. How did you hit?"

In the championship game at the end of my final year

13

in Little League, I had two doubles in my first two trips to the plate, both of them line shots into the gap in left center. When I came up in the last inning, my team was down 7–6. There were two on and two out. I got a fastball out over the plate and I swung from the heels. I caught the ball solid, the best feeling in the world. I watched it rocket toward left center, then watched it drop down out of the sky and over the fence. That had been the greatest moment of my life.

"I hit all right," I answered. "How about you? You play on your school baseball team?"

He nodded. "And football. Quarterback and pitcher."

I acted more surprised than I was. "Really?"

"Really."

After that neither of us talked for a while. The baseball went back and forth, back and forth.

It was the first time I'd ever used a catcher's mitt. I thought it would feel awkward, but it felt fine, and I loved having a baseball in my hand again. I could have thrown easy like that all day, but I sensed Josh was getting edgy.

"Look, Ryan," he finally said. "How about squatting down so I can cut loose a few fastballs? I haven't thrown hard in a while, and I miss it."

When you've got a bad ankle, going into a catcher's crouch isn't exactly your favorite thing. If it had been anybody else I'd have said no, but from the start Josh was different.

"I'll give it a try," I answered, squatting behind the plate. "But remember, I'm no catcher."

After the first two pitches I wasn't worried about my ankle. I was worried about my face. Josh wasn't fast; he was FAST. The ball absolutely exploded from his hand. The palm of my left hand burned, and it was hard not to back off.

"Do you think you could handle a curve?" he asked after he'd blazed fastballs at me for fifteen minutes or so.

I almost said yes, just to get away from the fastballs, but I thought better of it. "I don't know," I admitted. "I don't know if I've ever seen a real curve."

He stretched his arm over his head. "You'd better not, then, not without a mask." He looked at his watch. "I should get back anyway. Otherwise my old man will throw a fit." He paused. "Does that offer to help still stand?"

"You got it," I said.

▪ 4 ▪

Back at his house, Josh's father was standing on the porch, hands on his hips, frowning. "No more baseball until every box is inside and unpacked," he said before heading into the house. He didn't even look at me. Not exactly a pleasant guy.

But his mother was different. She looked like Josh, tall and dark with a long face and dark eyes. When she saw me, she smiled and introduced herself. She asked me about my mother and father, and whether I had any brothers or sisters. "Josh has an older brother, Andrew, who is at UCLA on an academic scholarship. Andrew is planning on law school when he graduates." Her voice was alive with pride. "We're hoping he'll come up to visit this summer, or maybe we'll go down over Christmas."

From the sour expression on Josh's face, I could tell he hoped his brother would never come up.

Once the introductions were over, Josh led me to the Ryder truck, jumped inside, and handed a box down to me. He picked up another one, and I followed him up the stairs to his room. From his window he had a view of Mount Rainier. "This is a great room," I said, putting the box down and looking out.

He shrugged. "It's okay, I guess. I liked our house in San Jose better."

"Why did you move?"

"It wasn't my idea. My mother is the brains in this family. My mother and my famous brother Andrew. She worked for Apple, but she's afraid they're going out of business. So when she got an offer from Microsoft, she took it."

"What about your father?" I asked.

Josh snorted. "He's a plumber. There are toilets everywhere."

After that it was work. Up and down we went, trip after trip after trip. When the last box was out of the truck and in the house, we stopped to eat sandwiches his mother had bought at the deli on Market.

While we were sprawled out on the porch eating,

Josh's father came out from the back of the truck grinning and holding up two wolf masks. "Remember all the Halloweens you and Andrew wore these? You two would howl and jump around in the front room, and your mom and I would pretend to be scared out of our wits."

"Just throw them away, Dad."

His father shook his head. "I'll stick them in the basement. They're not taking up any space, and you might want them someday."

Josh looked at me and rolled his eyes.

We spent the afternoon unpacking the boxes we'd carried upstairs. Josh had a ton of sports stuff: baseballs, bats, footballs, gloves, caps, shin guards, a basketball, shoulder pads. Most of it got shoved into a hall closet right outside his room. "There's one more thing I've got to get," he said when the last box was empty.

I followed him to the truck. Up against the back wall was a big cork bulletin board. It wasn't heavy, but maneuvering it up the staircase was tricky. Twice we had to flip it around.

Once we got the bulletin board hung up, Josh unzipped a portfolio, pulled out a stack of newspaper articles, and handed them to me. As he pinned the first one up, I flipped through the rest of them. The headlines were all alike. *Daniels Strikes Out Twelve! Four TD Passes for Daniels! Daniels Named Valley MVP!*

I stared at the huge pile. "You told me you played," I said, "but you didn't tell me you were the greatest athlete in the history of the world."

"I'm not quite that."

17

I flipped through a few more articles. "If you're half as good as these clippings say you are, you might just be the guy who can finally push Crown Hill High over the top."

He stopped what he was doing and turned to look at me. "What does that mean?"

I shrugged. "We have good teams, really good teams, every year. But when it comes to the championship game, O'Dea High always beats us. It's been like that for as long as I can remember. They end up state champions, and we don't even make the tournament."

"Really," he said, and then he went back to pinning up articles. But I could tell he'd taken what I'd said and filed it away in his mind.

I got up to go. "I promised my father I'd do some yard work. I'd better get on it."

"What about tomorrow morning?" he said. "You want to throw the ball around again?"

"Sure," I answered. "That would be great."

▪ 5 ▪

My parents were full of questions. What was he like? What were his parents like? Did I know what they did?

They liked my answers too, even the one about his father's being a plumber. My dad laughed when I told him. "That might come in handy some cold winter night."

I did the yard work, then went upstairs and showered. The whole day had gone smooth as ice, but something was bothering me, like a tiny rock in a shoe. I dried myself off, put on clean clothes, then went to my bedroom to listen to the end of the Mariners game before dinner.

The Mariners were up by two in the ninth when Albert Belle drilled a bases-loaded double to steal the victory from them. I flicked off the radio, then found myself wondering if a guy like Belle pinned up his newspaper clippings on a bulletin board in his bedroom. I smiled at the thought of a big star like Belle with his scissors out snipping away at newspapers, but then I looked up at my own bulletin board and I stopped laughing. Suddenly I knew what had been eating at me.

My bulletin board was half the size of Josh's. Pinned to it was a note I'd written in March about a history assignment, a birthday card from my grandfather Kevin, and a calendar that still showed May. The rest of it was empty. Completely empty.

I hate people who feel sorry for themselves. It's too much like making excuses. But there are times when I can't help but wonder what my life might have been like if I hadn't broken my ankle. Maybe my name would have been in headlines, like Josh's. *Ward Drives Home Three! Ward Homer Wins Game! Ward Leads Vikings to State!*

What makes it doubly hard to think about is that the accident was so stupid, so completely and utterly stupid. I was twelve when it happened. For two full years I'd been healthy. No ear infections, no bronchitis, no nothing. I'd grown six inches in those two years. I felt stronger every day, every minute. I guess I felt then like Josh felt now — that nothing could stop me, that I could do whatever I wanted, that the whole world was mine.

That was the spring when I hit the home run that won the championship. But I hit more than that one shot. I batted over .500, led the league in RBIs, and my coach told me I had the quickest wrists he had ever seen. I was going to be the next Ken Griffey, Jr. All you had to do was ask me.

July came and Little League ended. None of my base-ball buddies lived nearby, and school was two months off. I was bored stiff — until Brett Youngblood moved into the house on the corner.

Brett's father was an animal. He'd yell at Brett and his brother, Jack, yell and scream and shake them so hard you'd see their heads swing back and forth like rag dolls. It was usually over nothing — a bike on the lawn, the garbage not being taken out. Little things, but he'd go berserk. He never touched me, but I was terrified of him. I stayed clear whenever he was around, which wasn't often.

Brett's mother was a different story. I didn't stay away from her. She was younger than my mom. But it wasn't just that. She was different, too. Summer days she'd walk around in a thin white shirt. She wouldn't have a bra on, and I could see the outline of her breasts right through her shirt.

Sometimes she'd catch me staring. Then she'd laugh. "Naughty, naughty," she'd say, wagging her finger at me and smiling, and I'd turn bright red. Brett glowered at me when she did that. But I couldn't help myself, and his mother thought the whole thing was a big joke.

Brett was actually younger than I was, but he acted older. He swore all the time, and he was always talking about what he would do to this girl or that girl if he ever got her alone somewhere. I smoked my first cigarette with him, and had my first beer. I knew he was trouble, but he was also exciting, and nobody else my age lived on the block.

We mainly hung out at the Community Center, shooting hoops or playing catch or hitting baseballs. But some days we'd go to the forested part of Golden Gardens Park. That's where we coughed our way through those stolen cigarettes and choked down the warm beers. But we didn't smoke or drink that much — maybe three or four times all summer. Most days we just hiked the trails and climbed trees together. Typical stuff.

Brett was always the better climber. He moved through trees like a squirrel. He was fearless. In every sport — baseball, basketball, football — I could crush him. But climbing trees, he had me.

He liked rubbing it in, too. He'd scurry up some fir tree and throw cones down at me and laugh. "You wouldn't believe all the things I can see from here," he'd say.

I shouldn't have let it bother me. With his deranged father and his sexy mother, he needed his moment. I should have let him have it. But I didn't.

One windy afternoon in late August, Brett climbed way up in a maple. I want to say the tree was a hundred feet tall, but it was probably closer to fifty. Still, from the ground he looked small as he clung to one of the top branches.

"This is so amazing!" he shouted down. "This is the coolest thing in the whole world!"

I listened and fumed for ten minutes. Then I started climbing. I scratched myself up pretty good, and it took me a lot longer than it had taken him, but I finally made it as high as he'd gotten.

When I pulled myself up next to him, he looked pained, pained and angry. I didn't care. I felt as if big firecrackers were exploding inside me. There was nothing I couldn't do.

Then came a gust of wind, and the branches swayed. "I'm going down," Brett said, and a second later he was gone, moving from branch to branch, down and down and down.

The breeze didn't whisper through the branches. That's what it sounds like when you're safe on the ground. When you're up there, way up there, it sounds like groaning. The wind picked up even more and the whole tree started rolling. It was as if it were trying to shake me off its back like a wet dog shakes off drops of water.

I looked down. Brett was on the trail throwing rocks into the brush. "Let's go, Ryan," he hollered up.

"Okay," I managed to call back.

But nothing was okay. I hugged the trunk of the tree for all I was worth, hoping to find enough courage to begin. But the courage wasn't there. "Help me, Brett!"

Brett stood at the base of the tree, looking up. "What do you want me to do?" His voice was angry.

"Get my dad!" I shouted.

"I'm not going to get your dad. You got up there; you can get down."

I clung to the tree for what seemed like hours, but was probably only a minute or maybe two.

"I'm going home," Brett shouted up disgustedly. "See you later."

"You can't leave me!" I screamed.

"I'm not going to stay here all day." He started toward the path that led out of the park.

"Wait!" I called to him. "Come back."

But he kept walking, down the path and out of sight. I never saw him again.

I don't know how long I stayed in the tree. Probably no more than five minutes, but it seemed like hours. Finally I started down. The first ten feet were okay. Then came a long bare spot. I dangled my legs down, stretching to reach the branch below me. But I couldn't reach it. I was trying to pull myself back up when my right hand slipped. I clawed at the bark with my fingertips, clawed like a cat claws. It was no good. My left hand started slipping too. I dug my nails into the bark. I could feel the splinters going into the soft skin of my fingertips. It burned like fire, but I had to hold on. I had to hold on.

A second later I was falling. Not straight down. I'd be dead if I'd fallen straight down. No, I came down more like a pinball goes through a pinball machine. I must have bounced off twenty branches before I hit solid earth.

A woman walking her dogs found me. I don't remember much about her — only that she put her coat over me and then ran off, her dogs barking.

They drove the Medic Aide car right into the park. This man talked to me, felt my stomach, my arms and legs, and then with another man lifted me onto a stretcher.

I spent two weeks at Children's Hospital. Some of the nurses who remembered me as the Helicopter Baby visited. "Couldn't stay away," they joked.

I didn't get a body cast, though the doctors considered it, but I did end up with casts on both legs and my left arm, and with pins and a metal plate in my right ankle. My stomach was wrapped tight, and for a while I had to wear a neck brace, though I don't know why. My neck never hurt.

When I got home it wasn't much better than being in the hospital. I couldn't go to school; I couldn't go downstairs; I couldn't even make it to the bathroom. That lasted for two months. Sometime in there Brett moved away.

Then came the day when all the casts and wrappings came off. The doctors had warned me my legs would be weak and skinny; my mom and dad had told me the same thing. I just didn't believe them. I thought that happened to everyone else, but that I'd be different, that I'd pop out of bed and be like new — able to run and jump as well as ever, better even.

And then . . . there they were. A scaly, scrawny left arm. Two skinny, pathetic-looking white strings for legs. I couldn't run — I could barely walk. My right ankle ached. I couldn't bend it, and walking stiff-legged made my left hip sore.

I was depressed for a while, but then I came out of it. I figured all I needed to do was work and I'd be as good as new.

I did my physical therapy exercises, all of them, every day. And I got stronger and was able to run a little and do things. Only not as well as before. Not nearly as well. So I worked harder, tried harder, got down on my knees and prayed to God. But things that had been so easy and natural — running, hitting, throwing, and catching a baseball — felt awkward and unnatural.

And then, one day, I faced it: I wasn't going to make it back. There was no point in endlessly banging my head against a brick wall. For five years I didn't pick up a baseball.

Until Josh Daniels.

▪ 6 ▪

The next morning Josh was waiting for me. His front door opened before I made it halfway up his porch steps. "Good to see you," he said as he stepped out. He handed me a catcher's mitt and a mask and a little piece of sponge. "If you shove that in your mitt, your hand won't hurt so much." He grinned. "And you should get yourself a cup too, unless you don't plan on having any children."

When we reached the diamonds, I wanted to throw the ball right away. But Josh shook his head. "We've got all morning. We should stretch out first, run a little, get loose. Do it right."

I felt my body go tense. The stretching was okay, but I didn't want to run. He'd be too fast, and I'd feel like a fool. I swallowed. "I'll stretch out," I said, "but I'm not sure how my ankle will hold up running."

"It's that bad?"

"It's not very good."

Stretching has always seemed like a waste of time to me, but Josh was dead serious. Ankles, calves, hamstrings, groin, hips, torso, arms, neck — he stretched everything. I watched whatever he did and copied as best I could. The whole routine took at least half an hour. Finally he stopped. "What do you think? Seven, eight laps?"

"I'll try," I said. "But don't you stop just because I do."

It's about a quarter of a mile around both fields. Josh had long strides, but he wasn't churning his legs fast. My strides were short and choppy, but I was able to keep up. And my ankle didn't hurt — not at that pace.

We ran a lap, two laps, three laps. Slowly, probably without even knowing it, he picked up his pace. My breath was coming faster; my heart was thumping; my lungs burned; my side ached. As we finished our fourth lap, I slowed to a walk. "Go on," I said.

He ran backwards for a few steps. "You okay?"

"I'm fine," I answered. "I'm just going to walk a little."

He nodded, and I watched as he took off by himself. Free of me, he ran effortlessly, like a dolphin moving in water. As I watched him, memories of running — of pure, painless running — came flooding back to me. There was a time when I ran the way he did, when I could get there, wherever it was, faster than anybody.

When he finished his eighth lap, Josh put his hands on his hips and walked around the outfield in wide circles. He was sweating pretty good, but he wasn't breathing hard at all. Finally he came back into the infield where I was waiting. He picked up his glove, I picked up the catcher's mitt, and we started playing catch.

"You want to put that mask on and get behind the plate?" he said after about five minutes.

"You bet," I answered, crouching down and pulling the catcher's mask over my face for the first time.

That morning he played around with his grip, sometimes throwing with his two fingers split wide, sometimes with three fingers on the ball, sometimes with his fingers across the seams. The different grips made the ball move differently. The splitter dropped down, the three fingered job tailed in. About every fifth pitch was just pure heat, but even his fastball always moved a little. Catching Josh was like taking a ride at an amusement park — scary, but fun. The ball was there, and then it wasn't, dipping down and either in or away.

27

I'd always thought that being a catcher had to be the most boring position to play. Those two days taught me otherwise. There was nothing boring about catching Josh Daniels. When a hard ball is coming at you fast, and when it's dancing, too, every single nerve in your body is alert and ready. Your eyes are wide open, and the adrenaline is pumping. It's not a feeling you want to give up, any more than you want to get off a roller coaster. And Josh wasn't even close to pushing his limits. I knew he had more. Whatever more he had, I wanted to see it. I wanted to catch it. I'd have caught him forever.

Too soon he stopped. "That's enough," he said.

"You sure? I'm not tired."

He was tempted, but finally shook his head. "No, I don't want to hurt my arm, and you should go easy on that ankle."

We walked over to the drinking fountain. I splashed water on my neck and face, then took a good long drink. Suddenly I was on empty. I dropped to the grass. Josh plopped down next to me, then leaned back so the sun was on his face. We sat for a while, neither of us talking. Then he sat up.

"My old man wants to put in new copper pipes to the kitchen and bathroom. I've got to help him."

"That sounds like fun."

He smiled sourly. "Yeah. Right. But how about tomorrow morning? You want to do this again?"

"Sure, sounds great." Then I remembered. "Wait a second," I said. "I can't. Tomorrow is Sunday. I go hiking with my father on Sundays."

"What about the afternoon?"

"Yeah," I said. "If we're back in time."

■ 7 ■

Before I went to bed that night I set my alarm for five-thirty. Just thinking about getting up that early put me in a foul mood. But even if we were leaving at eight-thirty, I wouldn't have wanted to go.

The strange thing is that for years I'd looked forward to those Sunday hikes with my father. I couldn't play basketball or football or baseball, but I could walk. The Issaquah Alps, Cedar River, Mount St. Helens — we hiked everywhere. On Monday I had something on the other guys at school. "I hiked to Rattlesnake Lake," I'd say, and for a few minutes they'd be jealous of me.

But for the last year or so, the hikes have become a chore, something I do for him. The strange thing is I'm certain that in the beginning — when my ankle was so tight that every step was slow — our hikes were something he did for me.

It seemed as if I'd barely fallen asleep that night when my light went on. "Wake up, Ryan."

"What?" I said, looking at my clock. Five-ten.

"Cougar Mountain," he answered. "Remember, we're hiking Far Country Creek today."

29

I groaned. "I thought we said five-thirty."

"We did, but I want to get going before the trail gets crowded."

I covered my head with my pillow. What I wanted to do was to sleep until nine or so and then pound on Josh's door and play baseball. My fingers itched to hold a hard ball again. But I had to suck it up and go.

I rolled out of bed and dressed. I checked my ankle, turning it this way and that. Just a little stiffness. Downstairs I found my dad loading up his backpack on the kitchen table. He never goes on any hike — not even a two-miler — without double-checking his stuff. I'm sure it's because of what happened to my mom when the batteries went dead. When he was satisfied he had everything, he turned to me. "You want to drive?"

We stopped at Ken's Market and picked up a loaf of peasant bread and a half gallon of orange juice. Once we reached the freeway he pulled the bread apart and handed me a chunk. It had a good hard crust, and the inside was still warm. I ate it quickly. "You want more?" he asked and I nodded. He opened the orange juice and I took a swig of that too.

By the time we reached Issaquah the bread and juice were gone; the sun was just coming up; the air was crisp and clear. Little birds were jumping from branch to branch, singing up and down. Best of all, there were no other cars at the trail head.

Far Country Creek is a pretty decent hike. About a half a mile into it you come to Licorice Fern Wall, this amazing bank of ferns and moss that's got to be a couple of hundred feet high. You can feel the moisture, the incredible dampness. A quarter mile past that is Trog Swamp, another place that makes you feel the whole world is one moist sponge and that millions of little green plants are coming to life around you.

Beyond Trog Swamp the hike becomes a climb. Not a tough one, but it's uphill enough so that you notice. I kept expecting my ankle to give me some trouble, but it loosened up instead of tightening.

We climbed past the falls, and then up Marshall Hill. De Leo Wall is at the very top. From there you can see all the way to Tacoma, but it's spooky too. The drop from the wall is 600 feet, and after being in a wet forest, all that open air and sky makes you dizzy.

Once we reached the top, we sat against the buttress drinking the water from our canteens. A peaceful tiredness overtook both of us. So much air; so many mountains.

Then my father had to spoil it. "Have you thought about what you're going to do after next year?"

It's a question he asks all the time. I knew what he wanted. I knew what both my parents wanted. They wanted me to go to a four-year college, as they had. But I hadn't studied hard enough to get into a good school. Besides, I didn't know what I'd do at college anyway. There was nothing I wanted to study, nothing I wanted to become.

"I'll probably work part-time somewhere, and maybe take a class at Shoreline Community College. I'm not really sure."

"That's a good plan," he said, his voice flat.

I stood. "We might as well head back."

On the hike down we met lots of people. Some of them walked right by us as if we weren't there. Those I didn't mind. But others would want to stop and talk about how great it was to be away from people.

Things got worse when we reached the car. On the drive home we ran into a construction project on the I-90 bridge. All the traffic funneled down to one lane. I had an old Beatles cassette in the tape deck. As we inched forward, my father started humming along with it. His humming really grated on my nerves. I wished he'd either sing or keep quiet. As the minutes crawled by, I felt as if I was serving time in prison. I didn't want to be in a car inching along the freeway with my father. I wanted to be on the baseball diamond playing catch with Josh.

When traffic came to a complete halt on the west side of Mercer Island, I felt like screaming. My father opened a park service map and laid it on his knees. "We haven't been to Mount Wilsey in a long time. How about we go there next week?"

I couldn't do it anymore.

"I sort of feel like taking a couple of weeks off," I said.

He looked over at me, startled. "Something wrong? Didn't you enjoy yourself today?"

"Today was fine," I replied. "I just feel like a break."

"But why? There must be some reason."

"Why do I have to have a reason?" I said, my irritation breaking out with a vehemence that surprised me. "I just need a break."

There was a long pause. I could feel him staring at me, puzzled by my outburst. Traffic started moving again. Finally he nodded. "Sure, Ryan. Whatever you say. You tell me when you want to hike again."

When I finally pulled into the driveway it was nearly one o'clock. My father and I hadn't spoken for half an hour. "I'm going to make myself a sandwich," he said curtly. "You want one?"

"No thanks," I answered, even though I was starving.

Five minutes later I was at the Community Center with Josh. There were softball games going on both diamonds, so we had to throw along the sidelines. But that was okay. I was where I wanted to be.

▪ 8 ▪

Josh and I settled into a routine. Every morning we'd stretch. Then I'd run a mile or so with him and wait while he finished up. After that we'd toss the baseball around.

The first week Josh threw hard every day. I think he was afraid I was going to disappear, and he wanted to make sure he got as much out of me as he could. But once he knew I was in for the long haul, his routine changed. Most days he'd throw easy, not much more than a simple game of catch. Then, unless one of us had work to do — which wasn't too often — we'd hang out together in the afternoons.

It was peculiar how that worked out. I'm the Seattle guy, so you'd think I'd be the one showing him the city. But most of the time Josh decided what we were going to do. I'm not complaining: he picked good stuff. We went to Seattle Center, took in some Mariners games, walked University Avenue, saw the loggers climb hundred-foot trees at the fair in Enumclaw. But it was almost always his choice. Even on the days when we started out doing what I wanted, we somehow ended up doing what he wanted.

I wasn't the only one who went along with him. He had a manner about him, a breezy way with everybody that made things break his way over and over — especially with girls. Once we were down at the Key Arena the day of a Pearl Jam concert. Between us we had about five bucks. But about an hour after the concert started, he spotted a youngish female security guard by a back entrance. "Come with me," he said, a light in his eyes, and I followed.

The amazing thing is he never even asked her to let us in. He told her he was new to Seattle. It turned out she was born in Palo Alto, and pretty soon the two of them were talking about the boardwalk at Santa Cruz, hanging out at Great America, and rock concerts at Golden Gate Park in San Francisco.

"So I suppose you want to see this concert?" she asked.

Josh acted surprised, as if it was the last thing on his mind. "Sure. I guess."

She looked around, then stood aside. "Go ahead. Just do it quick."

We were by her like a shot, and we stepped inside the arena just as Pearl Jam took the stage.

Stuff like that happened all the time. He talked us onto the little golf course at Greenlake when we had no money. He got us into the IMAX theater with ripped ticket stubs. And I swear that every time we got ice cream at the Häagen-Dazs by Greenlake, the girl who scooped it gave him more than she gave me.

As far as I was concerned, everything about those weeks was perfect. But every once in a while I'd sense that for Josh something was missing, something wasn't quite right. One day when we were down at the Pike Place Market it came out.

"You know any girls who like to have some fun?" he asked, and the way he said "fun" made it clear he wasn't talking about going bowling with them.

You read about high school kids having sex. The newspaper makes it seem like that's what guys my age all do, or at least what they're all trying to do.

Well, I'm not. Not because I'm some virtuous guy who's not interested. I notice the girls at Crown Hill High, girls like Celeste Honor. I watch as they move in their little summer tops pushed out by their nice round breasts. I fantasize all sorts of things. But actually having sex with a girl . . . that scares me. I'm just not ready for that. It didn't scare Josh though. I don't know how I knew that, but I did.

"A lot of girls hang out down at the beach at Golden

Gardens," I told him. "I've never really spent much time there myself, but if you want to go . . ."

"Sure," he said. "Why not?"

So the next day we went.

There's an old brick building down by the beach. They have a teen activity center there, but as far as I know the only activity is standing in line to buy the junk food they sell. We bought a couple of Cokes and sat on a driftwood log. Not much was going on. A couple of volleyball games, little kids playing in a creek that feeds the Puget Sound, people throwing sticks to dogs.

"This is different for me," Josh said.

"What is?" I asked.

"Not knowing any girls. Down in San Jose everybody knew who I was. Nice-looking girls would just come up to me and talk all the time. I wouldn't have to do anything."

There was nothing I could say to that. Never once has some nice-looking girl tried to pick me up.

When the Cokes were gone, Josh nodded toward a spot down the beach where three or four groups of girls were sunbathing. "Do you know any of them?" he asked.

"I know who some of them are," I said, "but I don't really know them."

He stared for a little longer. "You want to go talk to them, maybe sit with them? You know what I mean."

I knew exactly what he meant, and a total panic came over me. The only girl out there I could have talked to was Patti Englert, but she was just a friend. She would have laughed in my face if she thought I was trying to make a move on her.

I took a deep breath. "You can if you want, but I wouldn't get anywhere with them."

"Come on. Don't sell yourself short."

I looked at my feet. "Really," I said. "Go ahead. I don't mind. I'd just hold you back."

He looked at the girls for a little while longer, then stood. "That's all right. Let's get out of here."

For the rest of that day I couldn't shake the feeling that I was a total loser, that I was letting him down. The next morning, when we were cooling down after we'd thrown the ball around, I gave him an out. "Look," I said, "you don't have to hang out with me. I'd still catch for you even if you, you know, if you . . ." I got all balled up and didn't finish.

He punched me playfully in the shoulder. "No way, Ryan. I like doing stuff with you. You're different from the friends I had down in San Jose, but that's okay. You're good for me. You keep my nose clean. I need that, because I don't want to mess up. I'm going to be the biggest phenom to hit Seattle since . . ." He stopped. "Has Seattle ever had any phenoms?"

I thought for a second. "Fred Couples comes from here."

Josh screwed up his face. "You mean the golfer?"

"Yeah. He's the biggest star from around here."

He smiled. "Well, okay then. I'm going to be the biggest phenom since Fred Couples."

▪ 9 ▪

As if to prove it, the next day he turned it up a notch. His fastball was popping, his curve was biting, and everything was on the corners, right on the black edge of the plate. It was exciting catching him, even though I still had the feeling he was holding something back. I didn't know what, but something. Finally, sweat dripping down his face, he waved that he was finished.

We sat down under a big oak tree to rest. The breeze was cool, and it felt good on my face. Josh looked at me. "You've got soft hands," he said. "Really soft hands. You should think about playing baseball again. As a catcher, I mean. Teams are always short on catchers."

My face went bright red. He was saying exactly what I'd been secretly thinking.

In a way it was a crazy idea. Squatting down in the dirt for two hours — that was the worst thing in the world I could do to my ankle. But in another way it made perfect sense.

Catchers don't have to be fast. They don't have to hit much. They have to have good hands, a good arm, and be willing to do the dirty work. Josh said I had good hands, my Little League coach had said my arm was strong. I was willing to do the dirty work.

"I don't know," I said. "I haven't played in a long time."

He shrugged that off. "I'm not saying you'd be All-League. I'm just saying you could probably make the team. We had three catchers on last year's team, and the third one wasn't as good as you. You should try out, unless there's something else you're into."

"No. I'm not really into anything. But trying out for the first time as a senior," I said. "Nobody does that."

Josh laughed. "That's what I'll be doing."

"It's different for you. You've been playing. But me . . ." I shook my head. "I don't know."

"Suit yourself," Josh answered. "But I don't see why you won't at least try out. You don't want to be a nothing, do you?"

He got up then, and I trailed behind him. But for the rest of the day his question kept playing itself over in my mind like one of those stupid jingles on the radio.

When I was alone in my room that night, I thought of the gung-ho kids at Crown Hill, the top students like Monica Roby. This would be the year they'd be hauling in scholarships to schools like the University of Washington or Cal Berkeley. Eventually they'd become lawyers and doctors and professors, and they'd drive fancy cars and live in fancy homes.

And I thought of the losers — the baggy-pants, drug-taking, gang types. Even they knew more about what they wanted from life than I did. They'd wangle some job in a wrecking yard or down on the waterfront or driving a taxi. Or maybe they wouldn't work at all; maybe they'd sell drugs or steal. On weekends they'd get stoned or drunk and ride around on their Harleys with other guys just like them. They'd have two wives and five kids and live in ramshackle houses with broken refrigerators on the side lawn, but they'd be themselves, exactly themselves.

Me? I didn't know what I wanted, or where I fit. While other kids had been finding out who they really were, I'd gone through my years at Crown Hill High like a hamster, popping my head out of my hole just long enough to scurry through the school day before racing back to my safe little room in my safe little house with my safe mom and dad. When I finished Crown Hill High, it would be as though I'd never been there.

I went to the window, and looked across at Josh's house. He'd left his mark on his school down in San Jose, and he'd do it again at Crown Hill High. He'd do it everywhere he went his whole life. He'd put himself on the line.

I remembered what he'd said. *You could be a catcher.*

It wasn't too late for me. I could put myself on the line. It wouldn't be everything, but it would be a step.

▪ 10 ▪

I didn't say anything to Josh. But the next day, when I settled in behind the plate, I blocked out everything but his arm and the baseball, and I moved fluidly with every pitch. I was better than I'd ever been, and that made Josh better than he'd ever been. It was as if we were one person.

He must have felt it too, because right in the middle of our workout he suddenly stopped. "You want to see my best pitch?"

All along I'd felt that he was keeping something back, that he had more. Finally I was going to see it.

"Sure I do," I said. "What is it?"

"A hard slider," he answered. "They're tough to catch."

"I'm game."

And I was. I figured I could handle anything. But I was wrong.

The frustrating thing was I knew what the ball was going to do. It did about the same thing every time. It would come fast, just like his heater did. Then, right before it reached the plate, it would break down and away from a right-hander.

You'd think that since I knew when and how it moved, it would be easy to catch, but that slider ate me alive. It looked so much like his fastball that I'd freeze on it. And since it didn't break until it was almost on top of me, I'd end up stabbing at it. Occasionally I'd catch it, most of the time I'd knock it down, but too often the ball would get by me and skitter to the backstop.

That first day I wasn't too discouraged, and I don't think Josh was either. But as the days passed and I didn't get any better, he started getting irritated. "It's going to break," he would tell me, his voice like a teacher's. "You've got to move to it."

"Yeah, yeah," I'd say, but soon enough another slider would get by me.

Those passed balls ruined everything. Instead of being in a zone together, we started fighting one another. Pretty soon Josh lost his rhythm. His fastball started sailing high and the curve didn't bite. After a week or so he told me he just wouldn't throw the slider any-more.

"It's no big deal," he said. "Don't sweat it."

But I did sweat it. I wanted to play, not just with him in the summer, but on the Crown Hill team in the spring. The fire was burning inside me again, and his slider was like water on the fire. How could I hope to be a catcher if I couldn't handle his best pitch? I had to catch it. I had to.

I still remember the morning. It was a little colder, and the ground was wet from a night rain. "Throw your slider," I said, pulling the mask down over my face.

He shook me off. "No, I'll stick with the fastball," he said.

I was having none of it. "Throw it," I said, my voice firm.

"You sure?"

"I'm sure."

Trust. That's what it took. Trust and a little courage. I had to put myself in Josh's hands. I had to move my glove a split second *before* the ball broke or I wouldn't be set in time. If the ball didn't break, or if Josh crossed me up and threw his fastball, then I'd get nailed in the throat. I had to believe in him.

He went into his wind-up and delivered. The ball came faster than I can think, but I did it — I moved my hands and my hips. It was a wicked slider, but it broke right into my waiting mitt.

Josh didn't say anything, not even when I caught the pitch again and again that morning, even when he mixed it in with curves and fastballs and changeups. We were back in that wonderful place again, just the two of us, only now we shared another pitch, and it was the best one yet.

When we finished, Josh put his arm around my shoulder as we walked to the drinking fountain. "I've never had a catcher who could handle my slider like that. Never."

"Thanks," I said, bursting with pride.

He stopped. "You're trying out, aren't you?"

There was no point in pretending anymore, either to him or to myself.

I nodded. "Yeah, I'll try out."

He grabbed my elbow and gave me a good hard shake. "That's what I've been waiting to hear. We'll be a team, me and you, like Steve Carlton and Tim McCarver, only better. Because we'll be like the Stealth bomber — nobody knows we're coming and *bam*, we'll blow them away!"

▪11▪

That was the day Josh met Monica Roby. She came walking down the pathway that separates the baseball field from the gym just as we were heading up it.

I've known Monica since kindergarten. I don't dislike

her, but I can't say I like her either. Not too many people do. Maybe it's just jealousy. She was born good at everything, and that kind is always hard to take. She's a straight-A student, acts in the school plays, edits the *Viper*, the school's humor magazine, and probably does fifty other things I don't even know about. I've never seen her wear makeup or any kind of fashionable clothes, but she doesn't need any help to look good. She's tall and slender, with honey-gold hair, crayon brown eyes, and skin that looks incredibly smooth and soft.

I introduced her to Josh. She was wearing shorts and a light blue T-shirt. As he nodded hello to her, his eyes went up and down her, slowly checking her out. Monica's eyes flashed. You just don't do things like that to her.

"You do anything this summer?" I asked quickly.

She turned away from Josh and spoke directly to me. "I camped at Salmon la Sac and hiked the trails. You ever been there?"

I'd hiked those trails with my dad the summer before. We talked a little about them, and then she got going about the incredible number of stars you can see on a clear night in the mountains. "It takes your breath away, doesn't it? It makes you realize how big the universe is, and how small we are." That was like her, turning a conversation about hiking into poetry.

Finally she looked at her watch. "I've got to go. Be seeing you at school, Ryan." She turned to Josh. "Nice meeting you," she said. And then she was off, down the path and off the field.

Josh's eyes followed her until she disappeared.

"Let me tell you," he said, drawing in his breath. "I'd like to know her a little better."

I shook my head. "I don't think she's exactly your type."

He looked surprised. "Why?"

I thought for a second. "She's not into sports at all. You'd have nothing to talk about."

He grinned. "I'm not really interested in talking to her."

"Yeah, well you'd have to be able to talk to Monica to get anywhere with her."

He shrugged. "Okay, so I'll talk to her. I'll tell her she's as pretty as the stars at Salmon in the Sack, or whatever that place is called."

I laughed. "Are you serious? There's no way she'd fall for a line like that. She'd laugh in your face."

He wasn't buying. "Girls are all the same. You tell them what they want to hear and they'll let you do what you want to do."

I've heard lots of guys say stuff like that. It makes them sound tough, as if they'd never let a female really get to them. Mostly it's just showing off. But there was something in Josh's tone that made me think he really believed what he'd said.

I wanted to set him straight about Monica, to explain her somehow, but I couldn't think how to do it. We talked about other things, but as we talked, my mind kept going back to Monica.

It wasn't until late that afternoon, when I was washing my father's car, that I remembered something that happened when I was in the fifth grade, something that explained Monica Roby better than words ever could.

We were out at lunch recess when a storm swept in from the Puget Sound. The rain came in sheets and the wind was so fierce tree limbs were snapping and telephone wires were swaying. The bell rang, cutting recess short, and everyone raced for shelter.

Everyone but Monica. Through the classroom window we could see her standing in the middle of the playground, her back to us and her face to the storm.

Mrs. Pavach sent me out to bring her in.

"Monica," I called, my head down as I fought the wind and rain, "you've got to come in."

She turned and looked at me then, and her brown eyes glowed. "Isn't it great!" she shouted.

"What?" I asked, trying to keep the rain from pounding me.

"The storm!" she cried, her arms sweeping out. "The storm!"

"You've got to go in!" I screamed again, and I grabbed her elbow and yanked her toward the building.

By the time I wrestled her back to class, we were so drenched Mrs. Pavach sent us both to the office to call home for dry clothes. "Honestly, Monica, I thought you of all people would be smart enough to come in out of the rain!"

For a couple of weeks everybody teased her. It was the only time we ever felt smarter than she was. But even then she'd been right. That storm was the most amazing thing that happened in fifth grade.

▪ 12 ▪

Those were great days. I wasn't just getting through the days anymore; I was attacking them. It was as if I'd had water in my veins for five years, but now — finally — I had rich, red blood.

It was Josh who had brought me back to life — Josh and baseball and the chance that I could play again. I was going to live and breathe baseball every minute until spring.

And then, one Sunday in mid-August, Josh stuffed his glove and a couple of balls into his equipment bag and looked at me. "That's the last I'll be throwing until January," he said.

I was stunned. "What are you talking about?"

"Football tryouts start tomorrow," he replied. "I'll have morning and afternoon practices, and a new playbook to learn besides. I won't have time for baseball."

I don't know why I was surprised. I knew he played football. I'd seen all his clippings. But still I felt as if I'd stepped on a trap door that had given way, and that I was falling, falling, falling.

I packed up my gear and we headed home. "Look," I said as we neared our houses, "shouldn't you still pitch some? To keep in practice?"

He shook his head. "The motion with your arm is different. It'd throw me off."

We stood around talking about nothing for a few minutes. Then he asked if I wanted to go to the Fremont Street Fair in the afternoon.

"I can't," I said, not really knowing why. "I've got stuff to do."

"Well, wish me luck," he said as we parted.

He was halfway up his porch steps when I suddenly felt selfish and small. "Josh!" I called to him. He turned around. "Good luck."

He smiled. "Thanks, Ryan."

I worked like a dog all day. I mowed the lawn, trimmed the laurel hedge, pruned the lilac, pulled up morning glory. After dinner I helped my father clean the gutters and sweep the hemlock needles off the roof. By the time we finished I was beat. I took a long hot shower and dropped into bed, so tired I fell right to sleep.

When I woke up Monday morning the house was empty. My parents had both left for work. I got up, went downstairs, ate breakfast. Then I looked around at the kitchen, at the dining room. The clock on the wall ticked noisily. It was nine-thirty.

I felt totally lost. I was so used to playing ball with Josh and then hanging out with him afterwards that I couldn't remember what I had done to fill the day before I'd known him.

I picked up the newspaper from my father's chair. I felt better then. I could kill a half hour, maybe an hour, figuring out the box scores.

But as I looked over the paper, I discovered I didn't care about the pennant races or the major leagues or any of that. Reading about baseball didn't do it for me anymore; I wanted to *play* baseball. But I couldn't. Not without Josh.

I felt like going back to bed, but I forced myself to go outside. I had no destination in mind, but after I'd walked for about five minutes I realized I was headed toward Crown Hill High. "Why not?" I thought to myself.

The football field is east of the school. From the sidewalk I could hear the sounds of practice. Whistles blowing, coaches yelling, players calling off numbers. I couldn't see anything, though, because the field sits on a plateau about twenty feet above street level.

I climbed the weedy embankment. When I reached the top I scanned the little clumps of players. They had broken up according to position. The running backs were dodging through cones; the linemen were smashing tackling dummies; the receivers were running patterns.

Then I saw the quarterbacks. There were three of them, and they were taking aim at a tire that was swinging back and forth from the goal posts.

I spotted Josh right away. It wasn't just that he was both bigger and taller and that his long hair stuck out the back of his helmet. I knew him from the way he threw the ball: the tight spiral, the incredible velocity, the amazing accuracy. All the skill I'd seen on the baseball diamond I was seeing again, only this time on a football field.

I watched for about ten minutes. Then I climbed down the embankment. There was no place for me on a football field.

I walked home feeling about as low down as I've ever felt. I moped my way through the rest of the day, the rest of the week. A couple of times I went over to Josh's house

49

in the late afternoon. Both times he was lying on the sofa, his arm wrapped in ice, studying his playbook. "It's different terminology from last year," he said, worried. "I got a lot to catch up on."

Both times I stayed only a little while. Both times he told me he'd come by sometime and we'd catch a movie. But he never came by.

My dad noticed I was around more, and that he wasn't seeing anything of Josh. "What's up? You guys have an argument or something?"

I explained about football, and how it was eating all of Josh's time. "Well," he said, "you've got your own life to live."

"Right," I answered.

The problem was that I didn't know how to live it.

Part Two

• 1 •

The night before school started, my parents went to a play at the Seattle Rep. Once they'd left, I sprawled out on the sofa and watched a cop movie on HBO. It was okay — a little sex, a little violence, a little mystery. I heard a loud knock at the front door just as this nice-looking girl started to run a bath.

It was Josh. "You feel like going somewhere and getting something to eat?"

I looked back at the television. Some maniac with a knife was creeping down a hallway toward the steamy bathroom. "My parents aren't home," I said. "We could stay here and watch a movie if you want. There's food in the fridge."

He shook his head. "I'd rather get out, if it's okay with you."

We walked up to Robertino's and ordered cinnamon rolls and mocha. Josh went down to the last booth away from everyone, which wasn't like him.

"My class schedule came," he said, pulling out a piece of paper from his wallet and spreading it in front of me.

I looked it over. "I've got Ms. Hurley for English too," I said. "And I'm positive it's fourth period. But I think that's the only class we've got together."

He folded the paper up and put it back in his wallet. "Well, one's better than none."

The food came. The rolls were sticky-sweet, and the mocha was tongue-burning hot.

"How's football practice going?" I asked.

He looked toward the street. "Not so good."

"What's wrong?"

He looked back at me. "Do you know Brandon Ruben?"

Everybody knew Ruben. He was a big kid, a shortstop on the baseball team and last year's second-string quarterback in football. "Sure," I said. "I know him."

"He might beat me out at quarterback."

"Brandon Ruben?" I said in disbelief.

Josh shrugged. "He's been here. He knows the playbook and he knows Coach Canning. Besides, ninety percent of our plays are handoffs to Colby Kittleson. He does that just fine. Last year I was All-League and this year I'm all-bench." He smiled wryly.

After that neither of us spoke. "Let's go," he said as soon as he finished. I stuffed the last bite of my roll into my mouth and followed him out.

The night had turned cold. Salt air was coming in from the Sound and big gray clouds were covering up the moon. We walked back quickly. "Look," I said when we reached our block, "the first day of school can be confusing. If you want we can go in together. I can show you where stuff is."

He shook his head. "Thanks, but Canning wants us in the gym at seven every morning to lift weights. And he's going to post the depth charts tomorrow too."

We'd reached his house. "Josh," I called as he climbed his porch stairs. He turned around. "There's no way Ruben can beat you out."

"We'll see."

"Really," I said, strangely sure of myself. "You're better than he is. You'll start."

He managed a smile. "Thanks," he said. "It's good to know somebody believes in me."

▪ 2 ▪

At seven-twenty the next morning I mounted the stairs and entered the main hall of Crown Hill High. I nodded and said hello to the kids I knew. And they nodded and said hello back to me. But I didn't hook up with anyone. It was my senior year, but I still felt like a visitor, like a stranger.

There's not much to say about the first three periods: math analysis, computer drafting, art. I won't even bother with the teachers' names. The classes weren't boring or hard or weird. They were just school.

Right before lunch I had English with Ms. Hurley. I

was looking forward to it, and not just because of Josh. I'd seen Ms. Hurley around the school. Most teachers are beaten down, but she glowed. She was from Egypt or Israel or someplace like that. Somebody said that in college she'd been a swimmer. Her olive skin gleamed and her dark eyes shone. Word was that she was excitable, that she'd get so worked up over a poem or a novel that she'd actually cry in class. Kids who had her liked her. I couldn't help hoping that something good would happen in her room.

I was one of the first there. I took a seat in the center, toward the back. I was just opening my notebook when Josh walked through the door.

"Hey, Josh, over here!" I called out.

He nodded in my direction, then shuffled over and took the seat next to mine.

"What's happening?" I asked.

"Nothing much," he said, his voice barely audible.

The tardy bell sounded. I couldn't talk to him then, but I knew what was wrong.

As Ms. Hurley took attendance, Monica Roby came breezing in. "Sorry I'm late," she said to Ms. Hurley, then she sat next to Franklin Dement, a tall skinny kid who acted in the school plays with her and who helped her with the *Viper*.

"Please be here on time in the future," Ms. Hurley said, but there was a smile on her lips. I don't suppose too many teachers are sorry to see Monica Roby walk into their classrooms, even when she's late.

Ms. Hurley told us her rules, then passed out our first

novel, a book called *A Farewell to Arms*. Once we all had copies, she sat on her desk, opened the book up, and started reading out loud to us.

The book seemed pretty good. It takes place during World War I. This man lives in a little village somewhere in Europe. From his house he looks out on mountains and a river. It should be the greatest place in the world, but troops are always marching down the road and he can hear fighting off in the distance.

Every once in a while Ms. Hurley would put the book down and ask questions about how it might feel to be in a war. The discussion was pretty lively, but I was only half listening. I kept sneaking peeks over at Josh. When you're used to a guy being fired up all the time, it throws you off to see him down.

The bell rang ending class, and we headed to the cafeteria. Josh's shoulders were slumped and his eyes were on the ground. We joined the line, slid our trays along, stopping now and then to have the cooks slop some food onto our plates. We paid and found an empty table in the corner. We both started eating whatever it was we'd gotten.

Then a little buzz ran through the cafeteria. I looked up. Celeste Honor, wearing a T-shirt with Mount Rainier blazed across the front, was walking toward us. "Josh," I said, glad to have something to talk about, "get a look at her."

Celeste is a legend at Crown Hill. She has an incredible body and she loves to show it off. Every top she wears is skintight. All eyes were on her — boys' and girls'. Josh didn't break into a smile, but he did follow her as she moved past us.

She slowly walked the length of the cafeteria before she sat down and her beautiful body finally disappeared from public view. You could hear the whole room sigh and the ordinary sounds and conversation of lunch return. Somehow Celeste had broken the spell of silence that had fallen over us, too.

"Does she dress like that every day?" Josh asked.

"Pretty much," I said. "Sometimes she wears less."

He shook his head and whistled through his teeth.

I took a sip of my Coke. "What's the word?"

Josh grimaced. "Canning posted the depth charts." He nodded toward Brandon Ruben, who was sitting at a center table laughing and joking with Colby Kittleson. "Ruben is starting."

I stared for a while, but then Ruben's eyes caught mine and I looked back to Josh. His head was down again, and he was mechanically shoveling food into his mouth.

"You'll get your chance," I said. "You've just got to be patient."

Josh didn't look up, but I could see his mouth contort. "Spare me the pep talk, Ryan."

"Listen," I went on, ignoring what he'd said. "All you've got to do is wait for your chance. If it doesn't come this week, then it will come next. If not next week, then the week after. I know how bad you must feel, but it will come."

I wasn't ready for what happened next. Josh's head snapped up and he glared at me, his eyes blazing, his index finger jabbing the air right in front of my face. "*You* know how I feel! *You* know how I feel! What a joke! I put every ounce of myself on the field every single day. Every ounce. And I've done it for as long as I can remember. But you — you get one injury and you quit. You don't know how I feel, so don't tell me you do."

I was so stunned I'm not sure I would have answered him even if I'd had the chance. But I didn't have the chance. He stood up so quickly his chair tipped over with a loud crash, and a second later he was gone — out the doors and into the main hallway.

The kids around me were staring. I don't know whether they'd heard what he'd said, or whether it was just the chair toppling over that made them look. My face was flushed and my heart was pounding, but I picked up my tray as though nothing had happened, walked over to the nearest trash can, and dumped it. The bell sounded. Everyone headed to afternoon classes. It felt good to blend in, to disappear.

I had American history and chemistry left. Mrs. Beck, the history teacher, had a bony, bird-like face and iron-gray hair. She peered down her glasses as she handed out twenty typed pages listing all the reading and writing assignments for the first semester. She told us ten times that she accepted no late work. "On time or zero! That's my motto." You could hear the satisfaction in her voice as she said the word *zero.*

The chemistry teacher, Mr. Woodruff, didn't look or act tough, but he didn't have to. Just flipping through the first five pages of that book convinced me I'd have some long nights ahead. But I was too numb from what had happened in the cafeteria to care.

▪ 3 ▪

When school ended, I went home and closed myself off in my room. I flicked on the radio and lay back and stared at the ceiling. Around four-thirty I heard the front door open and my mother come in from work. "Ryan, you home?" she called.

I went to the stairway. "I'm doing some reading."

She smiled up at me. "I won't disturb you, then."

My father came home a little later. I heard them talking together downstairs. He didn't come up at all.

I wanted to spend the whole evening in my room, but I couldn't have skipped dinner without facing the third degree, so I trudged downstairs.

My parents were both full of questions. "Your senior year! I can't believe how quickly the time has passed! Tell us all about it!" They wanted to know everything about my teachers — what they looked like, how hard and strict they were.

I couldn't work up any enthusiasm. Mentally I was back in the cafeteria, Josh's finger right in my face, his words striking like bullets. My answers were pretty short.

"Did something go wrong at school, Ryan?" my mother asked finally. "Was there trouble with gangs or something?"

"No," I said, shaking my head. "There was no trouble with gangs." I frowned. "I'm just not a little kid anymore, Mom. I don't like being checked up on."

"We're not checking up on you," my father said, stuffing a meatball into his mouth. "We're just asking you about your day."

"You *are* checking up on me," I shot back, working myself into a rage. "You want to find out about my classes. You want to make sure I do my work." I paused. "Well, I've never flunked, have I?"

My mother put her fork down and stared at me. "Pretty touchy, aren't you?"

"I'm not touchy," I insisted. "I just don't like being treated like a first grader."

Her face went blank. "If you don't want us to ask any questions, we won't," she said coolly.

"Well, I don't," I said loudly, and as soon as I'd finished speaking I felt foolish for making a big deal out of almost nothing. But there was no backing down. "I can do my work without you checking on me."

And to prove it I went to my room after dinner and started on Mrs. Beck's first history assignment even though it wasn't due for four days.

I'd been working twenty minutes when I heard the doorbell ring. I figured it was Greenpeace or somebody like that hitting up my parents for money. But then my mom called my name.

Downstairs I found Josh in the front room, a football in his hand, his lips pressed together tightly. "You want to go over to the Community Center, toss the ball around a little?" he asked.

It didn't take me any time at all to answer. "Yeah, sure," I said, even though I'd vowed never to talk to him again. "Just let me get a sweatshirt."

My mother followed me upstairs. "This is a school night, Ryan. What about your homework?"

"Oh, Mother," I said. "It's the first day of school. I don't have any homework. Besides, you just said you weren't going to check on me." I grabbed my sweatshirt and hurried past her down the stairs, and out the door.

I thought Josh was going to apologize, that that was why he'd come over. But as we walked to the Community Center we hardly talked at all, and what we said was nothing. Once we reached the field, we threw the football back and forth. His passes to me were on a line — hard, tight spirals. My throws back to him were lazy rainbows. It wasn't like baseball, where I was a real partner, but it was something.

At nine-thirty the field lights went off. There was nothing to do but go home. As we walked up our block, he spun the ball up into the air and caught it. "See you tomorrow," he said as I turned up the walkway to my house.

"Yeah," I said. "See you tomorrow."

I knew that asking me to throw the football around was Josh's way of apologizing. And it was okay, I guess.

Besides, what had happened was partly my fault. He'd warned me to keep quiet, but I had rattled on.

Still, nothing could entirely erase what he'd said to me. It was as if I'd flipped over a shiny golden coin and discovered the other side was all pitted. I wanted to flip the coin right back and pretend I'd never seen the other side. But some things are hard to forget.

After that we settled into a routine. I saw Josh fourth period and ate lunch with him every day that week. I talked to him and he answered, but there was a hollowness in his voice and a vacantness in his eyes.

I did have a run-in with Monica Roby during Ms. Hurley's class. We were talking about how a person finds out whether he is brave or cowardly, strong or weak. "There are times when each one of us is called upon to stand up for what's right," Monica said, her voice quivering with excitement. "We all face moments of truth. That's when we find out who we are."

Ms. Hurley nodded her head in agreement, but Monica's words didn't ring true to me. "You act as if life is some action-packed Hollywood movie filled with drama and suspense," I said. "It's not going to be that way. Most of us will go through our whole lives and never face any big moment of truth."

Monica's eyes widened. "Are you serious, Ryan? You can't possibly think your life is going to be that smooth."

"Well, I sure don't expect to spend much time defending truth and justice against the forces of evil and corruption like Superman," I scoffed. "Or like Superwoman."

I hadn't planned the dig at all. It just came out. Kids laughed though, and Monica turned scarlet.

"Nobody will ever mistake you for Superman," she retorted, but kids were still laughing at my joke, and hers was lost.

▪ 4 ▪

I'd never gone to any football games, not in my three years at Crown Hill. There was no reason for me to go to the opener that year either. Josh wasn't starting, probably wouldn't play at all. But when Saturday night rolled around, I knew I had to be there.

I took the Number Fifteen bus. Crown Hill kids got on at every stop, and by the time we crossed to Queen Anne the bus was rocking. Kids were hollering and shouting out the window. The driver kept looking in the rear-view mirror, a scowl on his face.

Inside Memorial Stadium, the dance team members turned flips while the yell leaders screamed: "We are the Vikings, the mighty mighty Vikings." Or: "Beat Franklin! Beat Franklin!" Even the band, which sounded terrible at school assemblies, was loud and lively.

The PA system crackled. "Ladies and gentlemen, welcome to the opening game of the Metro football season. Please note the following rules. It is against . . ."

Finally the special teams took the field for the kickoff. Everybody rose and cheered as Garrett Curtis, a big sophomore I'd seen in the hallways, fielded the Franklin kick and returned the ball to the thirty.

As Brandon Ruben led the offense onto the field, I spotted Josh, helmet in hand, standing behind Coach Canning, looking like a well-trained dog. Suddenly I was back in the cafeteria, Josh's finger jabbing the air in front of my face, his mouth spewing insults. *Let him wait*, I thought. *Let him wait.* It was a strange sort of revenge, and it surprised me that I wanted it, but I did.

Ruben's passes didn't have the zip of Josh's, but he wasn't heaving the football into the stands either. On our first drive we made three first downs before a holding penalty forced a punt. Our second drive ended in a missed field goal. Occasionally I'd sneak a peek at the bench. Josh was always standing right behind Coach Canning, helmet in hand.

The game was scoreless midway through the second quarter when the first big play came. We had the ball on our own sixteen-yard line. Ruben faked a handoff to Colby Kittleson, then dropped back to pass. The Franklin middle linebacker didn't bite on the play-action. He blitzed right up the gut and leveled Ruben, flat-out creamed him, jarring the football loose. The ball bounced free and a Franklin guy fell on it on our six-yard line.

Ruben popped right up, but he was wobbly walking off the field, and when he reached the bench he just about collapsed onto it. "He won't be back for a while," the kid next to me said to no one in particular. "Anybody know who the backup quarterback is?"

It took four downs, but Franklin scored a touchdown. Their fullback pounded the ball in from six inches out. With the extra point, they went up 7–0.

Curtis took the kickoff again. This time he broke a few tackles and made it all the way out to the forty before the kicker pushed him out of bounds.

My eyes were glued on the sidelines. Ruben remained slumped on the bench, head down and helmet off, still trying to shake out the cobwebs. Josh was going to get his chance.

It's amazing how quickly you can change. I'd been glad that Josh wasn't playing. I'd wanted him to sit and suffer. But once he was in the game, I wanted him to throw touchdown passes and lead the team to victory. I can't explain why I changed. I just know I did.

On first down he took the snap and made a quick pitch to Kittleson. Kittleson almost broke free for a big gain, but the Quakers' safety dragged him down from behind after four yards.

Second down was another running play — Kittleson up the middle for maybe a yard. That made it third and five — a passing down. I looked to the sidelines. Ruben was up, talking to Canning. He wanted back in. Josh was going to have to do something good to keep him out.

Josh took the snap, dropped back three steps, but before he could set his feet a blitzing linebacker was right in his face. He somehow ducked under the guy and came up firing. The ball must have gone forty yards in the air, a perfect spiral to a wide-open Jamaal Wilsey. It was a touchdown, a cinch touchdown — but somehow Wilsey let the ball slip through his fingertips. Everyone groaned. I looked back upfield to Josh. He was on his knees, his eyes to the sky in disbelief.

We had to punt, and the Quakers ran out the first half with a long drive that ended in a field goal at the gun, a wobbly thing that hit the crossbar and dropped over. Still it counted, and at the half Franklin led 10–0.

During halftime the bands came out and marched around, a light drizzle started to fall, and out of pure nervousness I ate two lukewarm hot dogs.

The way I figured it, Canning had to start Josh in the second half. Josh had put the ball in Wilsey's hands. It wasn't his fault that Wilsey had dropped it.

The teams came back onto the field for the second half. The Quakers took the kickoff, so I had to wait even longer to find out who was playing QB. They managed a couple of first downs before they had to punt.

I stared at the sideline. Josh and Ruben stood shoulder to shoulder. Canning looked at both of them, and a second later Ruben was pulling his helmet over his head and running out onto the field.

"What are they playing *him* for!" I shouted.

"The other guy didn't do anything," somebody hollered from below.

I was about to yell something back, but I swallowed the words.

Not only did Ruben play, but he played pretty well. We got a first down on a screen pass, another one on a nifty run by Kittleson, a third on a slant-in pass. But then Kittleson fumbled on a third-and-four and the Quakers recovered.

After that the game took on a boring sameness. Back and forth; back and forth. A couple of first downs, then a punt or a fumble. All that time Josh shadowed Coach Canning, waiting for the call. And all that time I stewed, hoping he'd get it.

It wasn't Coach Canning who put Josh back in; it was the Quakers. With six minutes left in the game, their safety blindsided Ruben on a blitz, hitting him so hard Ruben's helmet popped off. It was scary, and I clapped along with everyone else when Ruben stood and limped off the field, though I felt like a hypocrite. I wanted him out.

Second and eighteen. That's what Josh faced when he stepped up to the line. He also faced a revved-up Franklin defense that was out for blood. Too revved-up, it turned out. Josh long-counted them and drew them offsides, making it second and thirteen — a better situation.

He quick-counted them this time, and then dropped back to pass. The blitz was coming again, but Josh unloaded a bullet over the middle to Wilsey. Jamaal hauled it in and, with the Quaker middle linebacker out of there, turned upfield for eighteen yards and a first down.

Josh raced the team up to the line of scrimmage, calling the play without going into a huddle. He took the snap and rolled to the right to pass. This time he hit Kittleson circling out of the backfield. Kittleson took it in stride, juked a cornerback, and turned a five-yard pass into a twenty-three-yard gain.

On first down Josh ran a draw that went for about four yards, which I guess was okay, but I wanted to see Josh air it out. That's what he tried to do on second down, but before he could set his feet, their defensive end sacked him for a loss of six.

Third and twelve with the ball on the Franklin forty. Josh dropped back, looked left toward Wilsey, pump faked, then came back to the right with a long pass for Santos. It dropped down out of the sky right over the cornerback's outstretched hands and right into Santos's. Touchdown!

I exploded. Everyone around me did too. We celebrated as though we'd won the game. Then our kicker came on and chunked the extra point. I looked up at the scoreboard. Four minutes were left and the score was Franklin 10 Crown Hill 6.

Canning tried the onside kick, but the Quakers covered it. They ran three straight running plays, taking time off the clock. Our defense held, but after the punt we were backed up on our eleven-yard line with less than two minutes left. Along with every other Crown Hill fan, I was up and cheering, hoping for the miracle.

On first down Josh dropped a great pass over the linebacker to Kittleson, who pulled it in for fifteen yards. But Kittleson was tackled in the center of the field, forcing Josh to burn a time-out to stop the clock. He completed his next pass to Wilsey, who managed to get out of bounds, but it was good for only five yards. No way to win the game with little gains like that.

On second down Josh's protection crumbled. I thought he was going to be sacked for sure, but he straight-armed the first rusher, shook free of the second, and suddenly the ball was in the air to Wilsey, who had come open on the Franklin thirty-three. Wilsey was tackled immediately, and Josh had to use his last time-out, but there were still forty-two ticks left on the clock. The roar from the stands kept up through the entire time-out.

Next came a trick play. Josh lateraled to Kittleson, who lateraled right back to him. A pass to the end zone was coming, but a linebacker was right in Josh's face. He dropped him for a loss of nine yards. Even worse, the clock kept running. By the time Josh got everybody up to the line, there were only sixteen seconds left. He took the snap, dropped back a step, and spiked the ball to stop the clock. Third and nineteen, with thirteen seconds left.

You need luck sometimes, no matter how good you are, and on the next play Josh got lucky. He threw a lousy pass, his first truly lousy pass of the day. It was intended for Kittleson, but the ball hit a Franklin cornerback right smack in the hands. He should have intercepted, and if he had, that would have been the game. But the ball bounced off as though his hands were made of stone.

Fourth down.

Seven seconds left.

Everyone in the stadium knew the next pass was going into the end zone. There was no time for anything else. Franklin had four down linemen and seven defensive backs. Bethel Santos was split to the right, Wilsey to the left. Both were double-teamed. Garrett Curtis lined up in the slot.

70

Josh dropped back, looked left. Wilsey was covered. He danced around, looked right. Santos was covered. The pocket crumbled. Josh ducked under the rush, pumped once deep, then tucked the ball under his arm and took off.

He juked one guy at the twenty, broke a tackle at the fifteen, then cut back. Two Franklin guys overran him, but one guy had the angle on him. He hit Josh at the four-yard line, hit him, but didn't bring him down. Josh kept churning his legs until he'd dragged that Franklin guy into the end zone. The gun sounded as the ref signaled "touchdown." Six points went up on the scoreboard. Crown Hill 12 Franklin 10! We'd won! We'd won!

▪ 5 ▪

After the game I went straight to the bus stop, and I was on the bus before I even had a chance to think what I was doing. Other Crown Hill kids were staying at Seattle Center, hanging out. That's where the football players — Josh, Kittleson, Wilsey, Santos — would be. I could have pulled the cord, gotten off at the next stop, and walked back. But I didn't. I don't know why; I just didn't. Rain started falling. The bus's wipers squeaked as they slapped back and forth.

Back home, my mother and father were watching a movie in the front room, but they turned it off when I came in.

"How was the game?" my mom asked.

"Pretty good," I said. "We won."

"Did Josh play?" my dad asked.

"Yeah," I answered, "he did great. He won the game for us."

"Well, good for him," my dad said.

I started across the room toward the stairs. "Why don't you sit down and watch the movie with us?" my mom suggested.

I shook my head. "I'm pretty worn out. I think I'll go to bed."

I climbed the stairs to my room and turned on my radio. Around eleven the television went off downstairs and I heard my mother and father get ready for bed. There have been about a thousand nights when I've wished I could fall asleep as easily as they do, and that was one of them.

Around one o'clock a car pulled up across the street. I looked out the window and watched Josh get out and wave good night to whoever it was who had given him the ride. As the car drove away, he looked up. I was embarrassed, afraid he'd think I was spying on him. But his face lit up the instant he saw me. He motioned for me to come down. In a flash I was down the stairs and out the door.

A huge grin broke across his face as I met him in the street. "Did you see the game?" he asked.

"Of course," I said, grinning back at him. "You were great."

His smile wouldn't stop. "I told you, Ryan. Didn't I tell you? Didn't I? Didn't I?"

"You sure did!" I said. "You sure did!"

"Canning can't put me back on the bench now, can he?"

"No," I said. "No way can he do that. Not now."

For the next ten minutes he talked on and on, describing his passes, the final run. "I was in a zone. Oh, Ryan, it was the greatest feeling in the world."

I could have listened to him forever, but the night air was cool. He rubbed his arms. "I'm freezing." Then he laughed. "And I'm tired too."

An idea came to me. "The Seahawks are playing the Bengals tomorrow. You want to go to the game? I'll bet we can pick up some tickets cheap."

He gave me a thumbs up. "Sounds great. Let's do it."

▪ 6 ▪

I was knocking on his front door at eleven.

"Hey Ryan!" he said as he stepped out on the porch.

"You ready?" I asked.

He shook his head. "I'm going to have to pass. I called Jamaal Wilsey. We're going to work out at school. I'd like to get Santos over there too, but he's Ruben's best friend. I don't know if he'll come." He paused. "Sorry about the Seahawks."

"No problem," I said, hiding my disappointment. "It'll probably be a lousy game anyway."

I returned to my own house. My father was hosing the dogwood berries off the sidewalk. He stopped when he saw me. "I thought you and Josh were going to the game."

"Josh can't make it."

I went up to my room, sat at my desk, and started reading *Walden*, the next book for Ms. Hurley. I was on page two when my dad knocked on my door. "Can I come in?" he asked.

"Yeah," I said, even though I didn't feel like talking.

He took off his glasses, sat down on my bed, and started cleaning them with his handkerchief. I closed my book and turned my chair to face him. "What's up?" I asked.

"Nothing, really."

"There must be something," I insisted, "or you wouldn't be here."

He stopped polishing his glasses and looked at me. "Okay, Ryan. Here goes. I'm delighted that you finally have someone your age in the neighborhood." He stopped.

"So what's the problem?" I asked.

"Well, how to put it?" He breathed deeply, sighed. "Ever since football season started, you've been a lost soul. You're always looking across the street, hoping to see Josh. You're totally wrapped up in him, but he's got no time for you. It's not healthy."

"Is all this because Josh backed out on the Seahawks game?" I said angrily. "Because I can explain that."

His eyes went right to mine. "It's deeper than that, Ryan. It's always been there, right from the day you met him. There's something in your voice when you talk about him — something I've never liked. It's like . . . like you think he's above you. Like you think he's doing you a favor by being your friend."

I could feel the blood pounding in my head. "Listen, Dad," I said, my voice rising as the words spilled out. "I *am* lucky he's my friend. Josh has greatness in him. Do you understand what I'm saying? Greatness."

My father tilted his head a little and looked at me. "From what you tell me, he's got talent. That doesn't make him great, though. That's nothing but good luck. It's what you do with what you're given that makes you great." He paused. "You might find some greatness inside yourself, you know."

My mouth dropped open in astonishment. "Me? You've got to be kidding. There's nothing great about me."

A little smile came to his face. "I don't know about that," he said. Then he stood, and left the room.

He's my father and he loves me, but I hate it when he tries to boost me up. Only little kids fall for that. When you're ordinary, you know it. And nothing your parents say can change it.

Most Crown Hill High kids are pretty tough looking. You wouldn't think too many cared about something as old-fashioned as football. But come from behind to win, as we did against Franklin, and before every class it's: "Were you at the football game?" There was an electricity in the halls I'd never felt before.

I couldn't wait to see Josh fourth period. Because if I'd heard the talk, then he must have heard it too. I was sure he'd be in the stratosphere.

Still, when he walked in the door, I did a double take. It wasn't that he looked all that different, because he didn't. He looked the way he'd looked when I'd first met him, back in the summer. Eyes bright, shoulders straight, cocky smile playing on his lips and in his eyes. He was the same Josh all right. It's just that he was more Josh than ever before, if that makes sense. It was as if a bright light had gone on inside him, making all his features more vivid.

Before class started, about eight kids surrounded him, shaking his hand and patting him on the back and telling him how great he'd played. Rita Hall was so close they were just about dancing. He beamed and talked about how it was the team that had won, and not him. The bell rang, but nobody sat down until Ms. Hurley clapped her hands and called for attention. Josh sidled into the desk next to me and grinned.

That day we were supposed to discuss *Walden*. It was pretty serious going, and I wasn't in the mood, not with Josh glowing beside me.

Ms. Hurley talked about protecting one's "innermost identity against the onslaught of negative images," whatever that means. Most of the class tuned out, but Monica stayed right with her. The book somehow reminded Monica of the Miss America pageant and the clothes girls wear in beer commercials.

I didn't follow much of what Monica said, but Josh followed none of it. He was laughing and joking with Rita Hall. Once the two of them were giggling together while Monica was making some point. Monica stopped midsentence and glared at Josh. "Do you have something to say?"

Josh put his left hand on his chest. "Me? No, I don't have anything to say." Then he made a grand, gentlemanly flourish with his right hand and bowed his head as if he were showing her into a ballroom. "You go right ahead."

Rita giggled. Monica glared, then finished whatever point she was making.

When the lunch bell rang, Josh grabbed me by the arm and pulled me toward the cafeteria. "What's the hurry?" I asked. "Are they serving steak or something?"

"You'll see. You'll see."

After we'd filled our trays and paid, I headed toward our usual table. "Not over there, over here," Josh called, grinning wickedly, and leading me to the center table — Brandon Ruben's table.

My heart started pounding. "You sit there if you want," I said. "I'm sitting where I always sit."

But he was in high spirits. "No, you're not, Ryan. You're my buddy, and I don't forget my buddies. You're sitting right here, next to me." Laughing, he pulled me down onto the plastic chair next to him.

Jamaal Wilsey and Colby Kittleson came through the line and started for their table. When they saw us, they slowed for an instant, but then came over and sat down. Bethel Santos and Brandon Ruben came later, trays in hand. But those two stopped dead once they saw Josh.

"Sit down, Bethel, Brandon," Josh called, sliding his chair toward me. "We've been waiting for you."

I could feel Ruben's humiliation. "It looks a little crowded," he said. "We'll sit someplace else."

Josh kept at him. "Stay here, Brandon. We're a team, aren't we? We should all hang out together. Sit down." He pulled a chair out. "Come on."

Ruben looked around the table at Wilsey and Kittleson, who were nodding at him, encouraging him. Finally he sat down.

For a moment there was a tense silence. Then Josh scanned the table. "You guys all know Ryan, don't you?"

It was the last thing I expected or wanted him to say. Suddenly all eyes were on me. I nodded to them, trying to think of something to say, hoping that my face wasn't turning bright red.

Then I caught a break.

"Look!" Josh said, his eyes flashing. "Here she comes!"

Everyone turned to watch as Celeste Honor, wearing a purple halter top, put on her show.

"She is something, isn't she?" Josh said, when she'd passed.

"She is indeed," Colby answered. "My idea of heaven is a whole world filled with girls like her to look at."

That brought some comments about whether heaven might include a little physical contact. Nothing that was said was particularly funny, but I laughed anyway, glad to have the focus off me.

▪ 8 ▪

After that Josh assumed his place at that center table every lunch. Ruben, Santos, Kittleson, Wilsey — they came and sat around him as though he was King Arthur and they were his knights. They weren't necessarily happy about it, but they did it. I was there, too. I don't know exactly what my role was. A squire or a page, I suppose. But I didn't think about that. I was just happy to be at the table.

It wasn't only with the football team that Josh took center stage. In the hall, in the classroom, kids gravitated to him. "Great game!" they'd say, or "Go get 'em next week!" He'd toss his head a little and smile and say, "Hey, thanks." Sometimes, if a nice-looking girl was gazing his way, he'd joke with her a little. He must have done a lot of joking with Rita Hall, because by Friday she was leaning her softness into him in a way that made me stare.

I would have sworn that Josh was as cool on the inside

79

as he seemed on the outside. That's why Saturday was such a shock. He showed up at my front door around noon, and I could see fear in his eyes. "Let's go to the Center," he said. "I've got to burn off some energy."

As I laced up my shoes, he kept drumming his fingers on our coffee table, and on the walk to the park, he kept spinning the football in his hands.

Even when he was throwing the football he was off. He had way too much zip on the ball. It was as if he was trying to throw it through me. Finally I stopped. "Easy, Josh. You better save something for the game."

He sighed loudly. "You're right. We'll quit."

We sat on the retaining wall that bordered the pathway. "Don't worry," I said. "You'll do okay."

He looked at the ground. "Okay won't cut it, Ryan. I've got to be good or I'll be back on the bench."

"What are you talking about?" I asked.

"I'll tell you what I'm talking about. This is Ruben's fourth year in the football program; I've been here for four weeks. He's paid his dues, and I haven't. I'm stealing his job, and the coaches don't like it and the guys don't like it. I've got to be good right away or they'll bail on me. Fast."

He was exactly right. As soon as he said it, I knew it. And I also knew enough to keep my mouth shut.

Josh looked at his watch. "I've got to go. How about meeting at the Godfather's on Fifteenth after the game? I'm going to need somebody to talk to, and you're the only real friend I've got around here."

I nodded. "I'll be there."

▪ 9 ▪

I arrived at Memorial Stadium early. I wanted to make sure I got a good seat, high enough so that I could see the whole field, but not so high that the players looked small.

All around me Crown Hill kids were eating junk food and laughing together in the late afternoon sun. Stereos played rap music. There was a party atmosphere in the air. And why not? Cleveland was a weak team. And we had Josh Daniels, the new kid with the cannon for an arm, the kid who had single-handedly beaten Franklin.

I wished I didn't know how tight Josh was, how scared he was. Then I could have kicked back and enjoyed the last rays of sunshine and the music and the talk. But I did know, and my own stomach churned out acid by the quart.

We won the coin toss and Curtis carried the opening kickoff out to the thirty-five. On the first two downs Kittleson ran twice, picking up about five yards total. On third and five Josh had Santos open over the middle, but threw the ball high. Around me, kids groaned and then went back to eating popcorn and joking with one another. It was the opening minutes of the first quarter. I was the only one who was worried.

And I stayed worried, even though Cleveland didn't do much of anything. They were slow and small, and a first down was a major accomplishment for them. But throughout that quarter Josh couldn't get our offense into gear either. One drive stalled when he missed on a third and three pass in the flat to Curtis that even I could have completed. And the next drive ended when he fumbled the snap on two consecutive downs.

"They'd better put Ruben in pretty soon," a kid a couple of seats away from me said. "This Daniels is doing nothing."

The guy next to him nodded.

Josh was still at QB when we got the ball back early in the second quarter, but everybody in the stadium knew something good had to happen or he was out of there.

On third and four at our twenty-six, Josh dropped back and uncorked another wild toss that sailed over Curtis's head and out-of-bounds. Even worse, after he'd released the ball, he'd taken a vicious hit from a blitzing safety. The guy had stuck his helmet into Josh's ribs and had driven him to the ground.

For a long time, Josh lay on the turf, his hands cradling his mid-section. Canning hovered over him, and so did the trainer. Finally he stood, and applause came down from all around the stadium.

That's when I saw the yellow penalty flag. "Unsportsmanlike conduct: roughing the passer," the referee announced. Then he marched off fifteen yards.

You wonder about sports sometimes, about whether one play can change a whole game, even a whole season. Take that penalty. Say the guy doesn't cheap-shot Josh. We have to punt, and on the next series Brandon Ruben is playing quarterback. But those fifteen yards gave us a first down, and they gave Josh another chance.

He made the most of it, too. It was as if that late hit

had somehow knocked all the nervousness out of him. On the very next play he hit Santos for fifteen yards. Kittleson busted one for another ten yards, and then Josh hit Wilsey on the numbers for thirty-four yards and a touchdown. After that the rout was on. We led 14–0 at the half; 29–7 at the end of three quarters. The final score was 35–13.

Saturday night can be a tough time to catch a bus. I had a long wait for the Fifteen, so I didn't make it to Godfather's until nearly an hour after the game. I searched the place, but Josh wasn't there. I bought a large Pepsi, found a booth, and looked out the window. I wanted him to show while the excitement of the game was still in his blood.

The minutes crawled by. I finished my first Pepsi and bought another one. Still no Josh. I found an old newspaper and flipped through it once, twice. I looked at the clock on the wall. It had been two hours since the game had ended.

I chewed on the ice at the bottom of the cup. Fifteen more minutes passed. One of the workers came over. Did I want a pizza or a sandwich or another Pepsi? I shook my head. He wiped the table clean. I waited a couple more minutes, then slid out of the booth and walked home.

It was after midnight, so my parents were both in bed. I could hear my father snoring as I tiptoed past their room and upstairs to my own. I turned on the radio, lay back, and thought. I hadn't been up there five minutes when I heard a car pull up in front of Josh's house.

I slipped over to the window and pulled back the curtain. It was Jamaal Wilsey's red Pontiac Sunbird. A door popped open. Josh got out. He pounded the roof of the car with his open hand twice. Wilsey sped off, honking his horn and cranking up the stereo.

I won't say I wasn't mad at Josh, because I was. Who wouldn't be? Godfather's had been his idea, not mine. But I was mad at myself, too. Mad for being so stupid. Because I knew what had happened. I'd known it the whole time I was sitting at Godfather's.

You win a game and your teammates are your whole world. Your parents don't count; your girlfriend doesn't count; and some guy you threw a baseball to in the summer doesn't count. You want to be with the guys who played.

I pictured myself sitting at that center table of the cafeteria with Josh and all his football buddies, and I cringed. The whole thing was like one of those "What's Wrong with This Picture?" puzzles. Only this puzzle wasn't funny, because *I* was what was wrong. I was the fish flying in the sky; I was the square tire on the shiny new car. How could I have made myself so ridiculous?

I took a personal inventory then. Baseball was what I was pointing for, so I looked at myself the way a baseball coach would. It was pretty depressing. I was out of shape — slow, weak, stiff — not exactly the guy you'd build your team around. There was only one good thing. Baseball season was five months off.

▪ 10 ▪

The next morning I got up right away instead of lying around. I dressed, brushed my teeth, and cleaned up a little. When I got downstairs my parents were sitting down to breakfast. "You're up early," my father said, surprised. I shrugged.

My mother wanted to make me eggs, but I was in a hurry. I mixed up some of that instant oatmeal that tastes okay so long as you don't have it too often. My parents sat sipping their coffee as I ate.

"How was the game?" my father asked.

"Good," I said, shoveling in the oatmeal. "We trounced them."

"And Josh?"

"He was great."

"Glad to hear it."

I finished the oatmeal, took my bowl to the sink, washed it up.

"Have you got any plans for today?" my mom asked.

"I thought I might lift some weights," I said, "stretch out, maybe find the rowing machine and work out on it. That sort of stuff."

My dad's eyes lit up. "Good for you," he said. "Good for you. I'm not sure where the rowing machine is anymore. But I know the weights are down in the basement."

So that's where I went, even though I hate it down there. The walls aren't finished off like in most basements, and we've had rats more than once. It smells damp and earthy, and if you're standing by the furnace when the gas ignites, you feel as though a ball of fire is coming your way.

The weights and the weight bench were tucked away in a back corner. I took a rag and wiped away about a million spider webs, then I cleared a space in the middle of the basement for the bench.

Like most guys, I'd lifted off and on — mostly off — since I was twelve. And like most guys, bench pressing was all I'd ever cared about. I'd about break my back trying to heave some load of iron up, the whole time fantasizing about huge biceps, rippling back muscles, and adoring girls.

But that morning I lifted the right way. Squats, curls, reverse curls, bench presses — all of them with medium weight and lots of repetitions.

I lifted for about forty-five minutes. My muscles were so fatigued my hands twitched and my legs felt as though they had turned to Jell-O. Back upstairs I drank about a gallon of water, then went to my bedroom and got to work stretching.

I sat on the floor and pointed my toes toward the opposite wall. My left ankle curved easily, but the toes on my right foot were still pointed toward the ceiling. I could barely get that ankle to bend, and it hurt like crazy. Still, I held the stretch for a twenty count. Next I pointed my toes toward my face and held that for twenty. Toward the wall; toward my face. Over and over. Once the ankle had finally loosened a little, I rotated my feet — first clockwise, then counterclockwise — through the whole range of motion. When I was done with my ankles, I worked on my legs, my arms, my back — doing the stretches right, the way Josh did them in the summer.

After lunch my dad helped me get the rowing machine down from the loft in the shed. It wasn't so much heavy as awkward. An arm smacked me in the head twice.

I wouldn't have known where to oil it or what kind of oil to use, but he did. "You can keep this in your room," he said when he was satisfied he had it working as well as it could work. "Just shove it under the bed when you're not using it."

I thought rowing would be easy — or at least easier than lifting weights or stretching. I set the resistance pretty high, put the timer on for thirty minutes, and started. What a shock that was! After five minutes or so I was gasping for air. I had to stop and make the resistance easier, and at the twelve-minute mark I had to stop and make it easier still. I was laboring, but I made the full thirty minutes.

You always hear that being selfish is about the worst thing, that you should think of other people. That day I had thought about nobody but myself. And at the end of it I felt good, really good — better than I'd felt in a long, long time.

I got up early Monday morning and did pushups and sit-ups, and then stretched. I took a shower and planned out the rest of the day. There was school and weightlifting and the rowing machine and homework. And there were more sit-ups and pushups, and more stretching. In one day I'd gone from having nothing to do to having too much. But I felt good about it, good about making a commitment to myself.

In the hall before school I saw Josh. There were about ten people around him, so I went right by. But when he spotted me he broke free and came over to me. "Sorry about Godfather's," he said. "I got hung up."

"No problem," I answered.

Rita Hall playfully tugged at his sleeve, drawing him toward her. "We'll talk at lunch," he called. "I want to hear what you thought about the game."

Lunch.

All morning I stewed about it. I couldn't sit at the center table of the cafeteria, couldn't be the flying fish, the square wheel. No way in the world. I didn't belong there, had never belonged there. But I wasn't sure how to explain it to Josh.

Then, during third period, an idea came to me — library. I could tell Josh I had to study during lunch, and then grab something quick in the cafeteria in the final ten minutes before afternoon classes started.

It was a perfect excuse because it was true. I was falling behind in chemistry, and I had stuff for Mrs. Beck too.

Still, I was sure Josh would argue, that he'd tell me I was his best buddy, and that I had to eat with him.

I paid even less attention to the discussion in Ms. Hurley's class that day. Class ended and we headed down the hall toward the library. When we reached it I stopped. "I'm going to do some studying."

"Now?" he asked, his eyebrows raised quizzically.

"Yeah," I said, my throat dry. "It's a good time to get a computer."

He shrugged. "Well, see you around." And a second later he was down the hall and gone.

I pushed open the library doors and found a vacant computer station by the window. I turned it on, but I didn't even load up a program.

Everything had worked out exactly the way I'd wanted, but as I sat in front of the computer, I felt as if someone had taken a syringe and drawn half of the blood right out of me. All that stuff about my being his best friend was just talk. Not that the other guys — Jamaal or Bethel or Colby — were his friends either. Josh was like the sun, and the rest of us were like planets. We revolved around him. We got light from him, and we reflected some of that light back to him. But we were puny next to him. Unimportant. It wasn't his fault; it wasn't our fault. It was just the way it was.

At twelve-twenty I flicked the computer off and walked down the empty hall to the cafeteria. There was no line, but there wasn't much food either. I grabbed a turkey sandwich and an apple, paid, and then sat down in a corner. I took a couple of bites out of the sandwich before I looked out across the cafeteria. There was Josh, right in the center of everything, laughing and joking. I finished my sandwich just before the bell.

After that, every day was pretty much the same. I'd see Josh before Ms. Hurley's class. We'd talk a little, and then after class we'd talk some more. But when we reached the library, he went his way and I went mine. There was a solid line between us now, a solid line where there used to be only a blurred one, if there was one at all. I knew where I stood, and while that didn't feel good, at least it felt true.

▪ 12 ▪

The West Seattle game started at six on Friday. I hustled home from school so I could get my workout in and still catch it. I lifted weights and rowed. While I was stretching my right ankle, it suddenly seemed to come free, as if some scar tissue there had finally popped. It felt so much better I kept stretching it and stretching it.

I'd been at it for a while when I heard the front door open and, a minute later, my mom's footsteps on the stairs.

"Are you up here, Ryan?" she called.

"Yeah, I'm here," I said, opening my door and stepping into the hall.

"It's after six," she said. "I thought you were going to the game."

"I guess I lost track of the time."

She smiled. "Well, I'm glad you did. It'll be nice to have you home. We haven't had a Friday night together in a long time."

It wasn't bad either. My dad came home about ten minutes later. We three went out for pizza, then caught a Bruce Willis movie at the Oak Tree Cinema. There were no arguments at all.

Saturday morning I heard a loud pounding on the front door. When I opened it, I found Josh standing on the porch. "What did you think of the game?" he asked excitedly.

Somehow I couldn't tell him I hadn't gone, so I decided to bluff it. "It was great!"

"Oh, I was on fire," he said. "I could have hit a dime from fifty yards. Remember that one Curtis dropped?"

I swallowed. "Yeah, sure, I remember."

"Right in his hands. Right smack in his hands. I don't know how he dropped it. Still, five touchdown passes isn't shabby, is it?"

"No," I answered. "Not shabby at all."

"Have you seen this?"

He held the *Seattle Times* out in front of him. On the prep page of the sports section was a picture of him, arms raised, celebrating a touchdown. ***Crown Hill Crushes West Seattle 44–6!*** shouted the headline.

"The guy interviewed me after the game," Josh went on. "He says that if I keep playing like I can play, we're a cinch to go 8–0. And if we beat O'Dea in that last game, he thinks we could take the state."

"Beating O'Dea isn't going to be easy. I don't think we've beaten them in twenty years."

He punched me playfully a few times. "Well then, we're due, aren't we? Aren't we? I mean, they've got to lose sometime."

That reporter turned out to be right on the mark. Thursday Josh threw three more touchdown passes and we beat Nathan Hale 28–6. The next week Rainier Beach was the victim, 31–16.

It was after the Rainier Beach game that I gave myself my first real test. I'd been working out steadily for three solid weeks. The ankle felt better than it had for as long as I could remember, and even in three weeks you can feel your muscles harden from lifting weights. My stamina was better, too. I was able to row forty minutes without stopping and without sweating like a pig.

But I couldn't row around the bases or up the third base line to catch a pop-up or to the backstop to retrieve a wild pitch. If I was going to play catcher, I was going to have to sprint, something I hadn't done in five years.

That Sunday I decided to give it a try. I stretched my ankle for a good long time, then went to the Community Center diamonds and jogged about a quarter of an hour around the outfield. Nothing hurt — not even a twinge, but I wasn't kidding myself. Jogging and sprinting are two different things.

I trotted to home plate and positioned myself in the

batter's box. I imagined a pitch coming, a fat curve ball I could hit. I swung a phantom bat at that phantom pitch, and then took off down the line.

I meant to sprint. I really did. But I was so used to holding back that I'd forgotten, or was afraid, to run all out. I was going about eighty percent. No more. Three times the same thing happened.

After the third time, I walked the bases, shaking my ankle out a little. No pain at all. I returned to home plate, took a deep breath, and went all out, really sprinting for the first time in five years, stretching out in the last stride, trying to beat the throw from the hole.

Bo Jackson made it from home to first in something like three seconds. I wasn't doing that, not by a long shot. But I wasn't taking six seconds either. And nothing hurt. As I walked home, I could have sung with joy. Josh, for all his touchdown passes, couldn't have felt better than I did.

▪ 13 ▪

That was an amazing time. Everything seemed possible. Josh was living out his dream; I was getting ready to live out mine. I look back at those days now and wonder if I somehow could have stopped what happened later, if I should have seen it coming and done something about it.

But the little things seem harmless. Who can know where they will lead?

Take the lunchroom tables' being pushed together. I didn't see it happen. I came into the cafeteria the Monday after we'd beaten Lakeside 49–0 and it was done: three long tables right in a row. Every senior and most of the juniors on the football team were sitting at one of those tables. Josh was at the center of them all.

Moving tables is against the rules. It's got to do with gangs — with keeping large groups from forming. Whenever anybody else had pushed even two tables together, Mr. Phelps, the cafeteria supervisor, had pulled them apart. But Phelps looked the other way when the football players did it. You win six games and you get to bend the rules.

It was strange what pushing those tables together did. Josh and Jamaal and Bethel and Colby and Brandon had sat at that center table all through the winning streak. Nobody would have called them quiet, but they weren't out of control, or anywhere near it. But once three tables were pushed together, once five guys had become fifteen or twenty, everything changed.

There was some arguing, and a little food throwing, but it was girls mainly. Every time one walked by, guys would whistle or stomp their feet or hang their tongues out. Sometimes one of them would fake-grab for her as she passed, or maybe even grab at her a little, depending on who he was or who she was.

Once in a while a girl would complain to Phelps. Then he'd go over and tell them to settle down. He'd always talk to Josh. Josh would talk to the other guys, who would be quieter for a little while. But only for a little while.

Two weeks before Thanksgiving, Josh threw three more touchdown passes as we crushed Blanchet 41–12 to go 8–0. That set up the showdown game with O'Dea, the season-ending finale. The winner would be the league champion and would go to the state tournament as the favorite. The loser would go home.

Monday morning the halls and classrooms were buzzing with football talk. The football players roared to one another in the halls, roared and banged forearms and chanted: "Beat O'Dea!" Other kids took up the chant. All you heard was how we were going to swamp O'Dea, how this was our year, how nothing could stop us.

In the cafeteria, Josh and the other football players started a whole new thing. Whenever a girl walked by, they would rate her, screaming "Nine!" or "Eight!" if she was nice looking. If she wasn't, they'd get nasty. "Minus Two!" "Minus Six!" It wasn't that funny, but the whole bunch of them would howl and pound on the tables with their fists.

I was just bussing my dishes when Celeste Honor began her little walk. She was wearing one of those tops that are half a top, a little white thing that barely covered her. As she neared the football players, they started whistling and laughing and chanting "Ten! Ten! Ten!" and calling out other things too.

Celeste didn't blink. She strolled by, chin up, chest out, a little smile playing on her lips. As she passed him,

Josh stood and tiptoed up behind her, his eyes wide with excitement. He grinned at the other football players, and he put his index finger to his lips in the classic "Shhhh!" gesture. His buddies all went quiet. The whole place went quiet. Josh slowly reached forward, gently taking hold of the sides of Celeste's little top in his fingertips. In an instant he pulled it up. I saw a splash of pink bra before she jerked her arms downward, sending her tray and all the food on it crashing to the floor. She wheeled around and looked at Josh for an instant. Then her face turned bright red and she ran out of the cafeteria. The football players exploded in riotous laughter. Josh grinned back at them.

A second later Monica Roby was up in his face. "That was a real jerk thing to do," she shouted.

"Really?" Josh said, laughing and looking back over his shoulder at his friends.

"Yeah, really," Monica answered scornfully.

"I thought it was pretty funny," he said, finally looking at her.

"Well, you're wrong," she snapped, and her eyes bore into him, fixing him the way a hunter fixes his prey.

"Oh, is that right?" he shot back at her.

"Yeah," she said, still burning him up with those eyes. "That's right." Then she walked past him and out of the cafeteria, leaving him alone with Celeste's spilled tray of food at his feet and the eyes of the school on him.

Phelps finally showed up. "What's going on here?" he asked. "What happened?"

Josh shook his head. "Nothing's going on," he said. "Nothing happened."

· 14 ·

I did my typical workout after school that day. Normally it would have worn me out, but after dinner was done I was still wound up. I walked over to the Community Center. I needed to blow off some steam.

The field lights were on, so I decided to work on running from first to third. There's an art in catching second base just right, in stride and on the inside part of the bag. It can be the difference between being out or safe on a close play at third, but it's hard to do. Even major leaguers blow it.

I was lousy at cutting that corner, and I didn't get any better that evening. The whole time I was running my mind was going a mile a minute. I wasn't thinking about baseball; I was thinking about Celeste.

You could say she'd been asking for it, at least a little. Dressing the way she did, strutting around every lunch period — she liked the attention she got. She liked it a lot. But doing what Josh did, right in front of everybody, humiliating her like that — it wasn't right.

I don't know how many times I went over that scene in my mind. And I don't know how many times I ran from first to third. My mind shut off and I went into a kind of trance until a voice snapped me out of it. "Not bad!"

I looked up to see Josh sitting in the bleachers.

"How long have you been watching me?" I asked, a little embarrassed.

"Not long," he answered. Then he paused. "I didn't know you were doing stuff on your own."

"I'm just trying to get in shape."

"Keep going," he said. "Don't let me stop you."

"No," I answered, heading off the field. "I'm done."

"Let's go to Robertino's," he said. "We can get something."

I knew he'd searched me out because he wanted something. But it wasn't until we were eating that he spilled it.

"Ryan, what's Haskin like?" he asked, his voice soft.

"Haskin? You mean the principal?"

"Yeah. Him. What's he like?"

"I don't know. I've never spoken a word to him. Why?"

Josh frowned. "He left a message on the answering machine. He wants to meet with me and my parents tomorrow." He paused. "You were in the cafeteria today, weren't you?"

"Sure. I was there."

"You don't think he'd suspend me, do you? He wouldn't do that, not with the O'Dea game this weekend. I mean, he wants to win too, don't you think?"

"I don't think he'll suspend you," I said, "but I don't know for sure."

He frowned. "It was your friend Monica Roby who made a stink about it, you know."

My chest tightened. I felt as though he was somehow blaming me. "You did a dumb thing, Josh. And I warned you about her."

He scowled. "I think about that first time I saw Monica and how I was going to move on her. What a joke!"

We sat for a while, both of us thinking of the summer, neither of us saying anything. "Let's go home," Josh said at last.

When I stepped into Ms. Hurley's classroom the next morning, I looked for Josh. He wasn't there. Every time the door opened my eyes shot over to it. But when the tardy bell rang, Josh's desk was still empty. Ms. Hurley took roll, and then she started talking about *Walden* and how Thoreau moved out of his house and into a cabin in the woods because there was too much junk cluttering up his life.

She asked us to consider what clutters up our lives, and a million things came to my mind. Television, radio, billboards, 7-Elevens, clothes, shoes, magazines, books. It suddenly seemed to me that almost everything in the world was junk.

I was about to raise my hand when the door opened. Josh stepped quickly up to the front of the room, handed Ms. Hurley a pass, and then took his seat next to me.

"Everything okay?" I whispered.

He rolled his hand back and forth in front of him in

a gesture that meant "so-so." Then he slumped into his seat.

I kept peeking at the clock, waiting for the end of the hour when we could really talk. With ten minutes left in class, Ms. Hurley passed out discussion questions. "Form small groups and talk about these among yourselves."

I pulled up next to Josh. "Tell me what happened."

He shrugged. "Haskin gave me a lecture. My old man gave me a lecture. My mother gave me a lecture. Coach Canning gave me a lecture. I told them all I was sorry. Then Haskin told me I couldn't eat in the cafeteria for a month and that I had to write a letter of apology to Celeste."

I was amazed. "Nothing else? Just a letter?"

He frowned. "Canning made some noises about sitting me down on Saturday, but —" He stopped midsentence. Monica Roby was looking at him. "Disappointed?" His voice was challenging. "Did you think they were going to expel me?"

"I don't know what you're talking about," she said.

"Don't act innocent. You reported me. I know it."

She laughed scornfully. "I didn't report you."

"Yes, you did," he said with conviction.

"Listen," she answered. "I'm not sorry that someone reported you. And if I'd thought about it, I might have done it. But it wasn't me."

He pointed his finger at her. "You did it and I know it."

She sniggered. "You can believe what you want to believe. I don't really care."

School was different the rest of the week. Teachers patrolled the halls, making sure nobody started with the "Beat O'Dea" cheer. In classroom after classroom we got the standard pep talk about how academics come first and how football is only a game. The cafeteria was strangely quiet too. Josh wasn't there; tables weren't pushed together. The other football players ate in small, scattered groups.

In the hallways kids talked about the "Celeste thing." Most thought the whole incident was a joke, but some — especially some of the girls — were pretty hot about it. "The whole bunch of them are animals." "They treat girls like things, not people." You heard that sort of stuff.

Nobody ever asked me what I thought. I suppose everyone figured I was on Josh's side. But I'm not sure I would have defended him if anybody had ever asked. I'm not sure what I would have said.

▪ 15 ▪

And then it was O'Dea. The championship game. In the stands before the kickoff you heard one thing. Was this the year? Was this finally the year that it was our turn?

We won the toss and received the opening kickoff. It was a squib kick that one of our upfield guys handled on a bounce. He cradled it in both arms and returned it to the thirty-three before they brought him down.

As the offense trotted on the field, a murmur went through the crowd. Brandon Ruben was at quarterback.

Then the questions really came. "Is Daniels hurt or something?" . . . "What's Ruben doing out there?" . . . "It's not because of that Celeste thing, is it?" . . . "Is he going to play the whole game?"

On his first pass attempt, Ruben got crunched just as he released the ball by Number Forty, a big, quick linebacker I'd noticed during warm-ups. The pass floated out into the flat, a dying quail. An O'Dea safety intercepted it on the dead run, and before anyone had even settled into his seat, the safety was crossing the goal line. Touchdown O'Dea.

I looked back upfield to Ruben. He was down on one knee, the wind knocked out of him. Kittleson was helping him up.

O'Dea kicked off again, and again Ruben had a rough series. He fumbled one snap, only to recover it himself. On third and eight he misfired on a quick pass over the middle. Number Forty leveled him again right after he released the ball. I'm sure Ruben was glad to see our punter come onto the field and kick the ball away.

There was nothing fancy about O'Dea's game plan. They used the I-formation, and they pounded the ball right down our throats. They had two tailbacks — both of whom were big and fast. One guy would run the ball for three or four downs, then go to the sidelines for a blow while the other guy came in and racked up the yardage. Watching their offense cut through our defense was like watching a tank roll over a doghouse.

They drove all the way to our six-yard line — every yard gained on the ground. On first down, their quarterback faked a handoff. All our defensive players bit, shooting the gaps to try to stop the run. Their tight end slipped into the end zone. There was no one within ten yards of him when he pulled in the pass. Six minutes into the game we were down 14–0.

The rest of the first half was a nightmare. It was Ruben, Ruben, Ruben — the guy who couldn't win. And all the time you could see Josh — the guy who could — standing there, itching to play. When the score reached 24–0, the chanting started: "We want Daniels! We want Daniels! We want Daniels!"

At halftime everybody had it figured out. Josh was sure to start the second half. Canning had made his point, but enough was enough. Twenty-four points was a ton of points, but if anyone could bring us back, it was Josh.

But when our offense came on the field in the third quarter, Brandon Ruben was still running the team.

The O'Dea guys were really teeing off on him. They were overpowering our linemen, just annihilating them. Ruben would take a three-step drop and have about a tenth of a second to throw before some guy was right in his face.

The score was still 24–0 with about four minutes left in the third quarter when it happened. Ruben had gotten rid of the ball when Number Forty drove him into the ground. From where I was you could see Ruben's head hit the turf and bounce up. It took about five minutes for Ruben to get up, and it took two guys to help him off the field. Everybody was up and clapping for him, glad to see him moving.

As Ruben was helped off, Josh trotted on. The applause for Ruben blended with the cheers for Josh, and suddenly the Crown Hill section was alive again. It was only the third quarter. There was plenty of time for Josh to bring us back. He was the miracle worker, the guy who'd turned the season around. Turning a game around would be a snap.

On his first play he threw a little hitch pass over the middle. Before Santos could pull it in, the O'Dea safety hit him and the ball was jarred loose. That made it third and ten.

Josh took the snap and rolled to the right to buy some time. But the blitz was on, and before anybody came open, he had to unload. The pass sailed out-of-bounds, and our punter came on.

I sat back, trying to stay confident. Josh just needed to get the feel of the game, to get loose. Then he'd work his magic.

But O'Dea took the punt and came after us again, grinding up great big chunks of yardage on the ground and taking precious time off the clock. Four yards. Seven yards. Five yards. Nine yards. Down the field and into the end zone. 31–0.

It was over. Not even Josh could bring us back from

that deficit. The smart thing to do was to pack it in, to run some sweeps or maybe some short passes.

After what happened later that year, lots of people say that Josh was a coward. They say that only a coward would do what he did. But I don't see how anybody who saw Josh play the fourth quarter of that game could ever think it was that simple. Because what Josh showed that day was courage. Pure courage.

Nobody else seemed to be even trying. Santos had pulled himself from the game. Wilsey was just going through the motions. But Josh wouldn't quit. The O'Dea guys teed off on him every down. Still he'd hold the ball and hold the ball, not letting it go until the last possible second, and then taking the hard shots that came. Time after time Number Forty drilled him. Time after time Josh picked himself up off the turf.

With three minutes left in the game, Josh put a drive together. It was all pride — *his* pride. O'Dea led 38–0 by then. But that zero sitting up on the scoreboard was the ultimate humiliation.

A sophomore wide receiver, Andrew Hanson, had replaced Santos. Hanson had fresh legs, and he wanted to show what he could do. Josh hit him with two deep outs in a row. That put the ball on the O'Dea thirty-three. Then we picked up fifteen yards on an unsportsmanlike conduct penalty for a late hit. With under a minute left in the game, we had a first down on the O'Dea eighteen.

The clock was running as Josh hurried the team up to the line. Even though the game had been decided, you could feel the tension. O'Dea wanted the shutout as much as Josh wanted to keep them from getting it. He dropped back to pass — an all-out blitz was coming. Just as he unloaded the ball, one O'Dea guy hit him low while Number Forty blasted him straight on. Josh went down hard, his head smacking the turf just as Ruben's had.

But his pass was a thing of beauty. Hanson had run a fade pattern into the corner of the end zone, and the ball dropped out of the sky and into his outstretched hands for a touchdown. There would be no league championship, no berth in the state championship tournament. But we hadn't been shut out.

Sunday morning I went over to Josh's house. His mother let me in. "He's on the sofa in the den," she said, her face gray. She paused. "You're smart not to play football, Ryan."

I was stunned when I saw him. He was lying on the sofa under about a dozen blankets. His whole face was swollen. He had an ice pack on his neck and another one on his right shoulder. He looked as though he'd gone twelve rounds against Mike Tyson.

"Hey, Ryan," he murmured. "What's up?" Even his voice was off — raspy and clotted.

"Nothing much. I just wanted to come by and see how you are."

He smiled, and I could tell that even that hurt. "I'm terrific. Never been better."

The television was on to the 49ers–Eagles game. I watched for a few minutes. When I looked over at him, his eyes were almost closed. "Listen," I said, "I'll be taking off now. You rest up. I'll see you tomorrow at school."

He shook his head. "I doubt I'll make it tomorrow. Not unless I feel a whole lot better." He paused. "But come over tomorrow night. We can watch Monday Night Football."

"You got it," I replied.

I left, stunned. I don't know why. I'd seen it all. The crushing tackles, the blind-side hits. In the movies guys shrug off beatings as if they are pillow fights, but real life isn't a movie. Josh wasn't Superman. I banged my head a couple of times with the heel of my hand. There are times when my own stupidity amazes me.

▪ 16 ▪

Nobody mentioned the football game at school on Monday. It was as if it had all been a bad dream that no one wanted to talk about. The halls were quiet; the posters were down. Everything was back to normal.

In English Ms. Hurley had us read a short story about some guy with two doors in front of him. Behind one door was a lady and behind the other was a tiger, or something like that. I read the thing beginning to end, but I just read words. I didn't follow it at all.

The discussion never got going. Even Monica was strangely quiet. A couple of times I caught her sneaking peeks at Josh's empty desk. For a while I wondered if somehow she'd heard what a beating he'd taken and felt sorry for him, but that made no sense.

Just before the dismissal bell, Ms. Hurley clapped her hands to get our attention. "I almost forgot," she said, holding up a stack of papers. "A new issue of the *Viper* is out. Monica and Franklin and many others worked hard on it. So please don't take it if you're just going to throw it away."

I grabbed a copy on my way out the door. I headed to the computer lab, where I finished up some end-of-the-chapter questions for history class. As I waited for the printer, I pulled out the *Viper* and flipped through it.

The main story made fun of Mr. Hagstrom, a French teacher who was notorious for talking too much about his Brittany spaniel, Buddy. Then there was a sci-fi/fantasy thing about how the school's water was tainted with some strange chemical that made everyone live their lives in reverse. Adults were sucking their thumbs and wetting their pants while babies were driving cars and reading Shakespeare. Maybe it was funny and I just wasn't in the mood, but I was about to toss the whole thing when a short piece on the last page caught my eye.

Jocko Come Home

PLEASE HELP! Our beloved dog, Jocko Spaniel, is missing. Jocko is a fun-loving hound who loves to roll on the ground with boys. Around girls, Jocko slobbers uncon-

trollably and howls. If you find him, please call 1-800-Clueless. P.S. Jocko desperately needs neutering!

It was playing dirty, pure and simple. All afternoon I seethed. When the dismissal bell rang, I went to the front steps and looked everywhere for Monica. I was always running into her around the school, but the one time I wanted to see her she was nowhere to be found.

Then it hit me. She'd be in the publishing center, a little room in back of the stage. That's where the staff of the *Viper* met, and I'd heard Franklin say something about a party.

I walked down the hall to the theater. The main lights were off, but I could hear laughter coming from behind the black curtain that was pulled across the stage. I strode down the center aisle, hopped onto the stage, and pulled the curtains apart. There were six of them, Monica and Franklin and Linda Marsh and some freshmen and sophomores I didn't know, sitting at a long table eating cupcakes and drinking Coke and talking. Everyone stopped when they saw me.

"That was a cheap shot, Monica," I said.

"What are you talking about?" she asked.

"You know exactly what I'm talking about. Josh didn't deserve that, not after what he's done for this school."

She smiled her know-it-all smile. " 'After what he has done for the school,' " she echoed, looking at her friends. "Tell me, Ryan, what *is* it that he has done for this school?"

"Maybe you didn't notice," I said, "but he's given us

109

something to be proud of, some reason to be glad we go to Crown Hill High."

She continued smiling sarcastically. "Oh, I am so delighted to go to a school where the jocks sit together in the center of the cafeteria hooting at girls and copping cheap feels. My heart swells with pride!"

"I wasn't talking about that."

Her smile disappeared. She picked up a *Viper* and waved it in front of me. "Well, that's what I was talking about."

I felt the ground slipping away from me. "Other guys were louder and grosser than Josh, and you know it."

She glared. "What about Celeste Honor? Was that some other guy too?"

"Come off it," I said. "Celeste has been asking for something like that for years. He was just joking around."

Monica tilted her head. The smug smile returned. "Well, that's all I was doing, Ryan. Just joking around. If you can dish it out, you've got to be able to take it. Isn't that what guys always say?"

I stood there, suddenly feeling stupid. I needed to come up with some answer, but I couldn't think of anything. I swallowed, then I turned and walked away. The heavy curtains rustled as they closed behind me. When I walked out of the theater, I could hear the whole bunch of them laughing.

• 17 •

A guy is lying on his sofa, beat up and bruised. His head is aching, his face is puffy, and every muscle and bone in his body hurts. He's just come up empty in the biggest game of his life, and you've got to tell him that the school magazine makes him out to be an idiot and a pervert. There's a fun job.

Actually I didn't describe the article. I sat in the big chair next to him and watched the opening of the Cowboys–Raiders game on Monday Night Football. When the first set of commercials came on, I handed the *Viper* to him.

"Monica Roby," I said.

He looked puzzled, then he read the words I'd circled. "This is stupid," he said, throwing it back to me.

"That's exactly what it is," I replied, and I started to shove it into my back pocket.

He grabbed it back. "Let me read it again." His jaw tightened as he read. "This is something my brother would think was funny. I know her type. She thinks she's so clever and smart and everybody else is dumb."

I watched a beer commercial. A little time ticked away.

"You know what I'd do if I were you?" I said. "I'd just forget about it. Act like it never happened. That would show her."

His eyes widened. "No way, Ryan. Absolutely no way. I'll get even with her. I don't know how, but I will."

We watched the game then, both of us silent. Emmitt Smith was running wild, breaking tackles and scoring touchdowns. At halftime I got us some Cokes from his refrigerator.

"You know," he said as he drank his off, "she cost us the game."

I put my Coke down. "What are you talking about?"

"I mean that if I had started, we'd have won."

I thought of how much bigger the O'Dea guys were, and how their offense had cut right through our defense. "The game would have been closer, but they were —"

"They were nothing," he interrupted, his tone vehement. "Nothing. Ruben made them look good. I'm telling you, I could have beaten them."

On the television Dallas was celebrating another touchdown. I got up and stretched my arms over my head. "I'll be going home now," I said. "You coming to school tomorrow?"

He shook his head. "My mother made me go see a doctor. He wants me to take the week off, which is okay by me. I won't go back until after Thanksgiving."

It was actually good Josh stayed away. Tuesday morning in the halls I saw kids pointing to the *Viper* and laughing. But by Tuesday afternoon most copies were in garbage cans. Wednesday was a half day. Everyone was looking forward to the time off from school. Josh, Monica, the *Viper* — they were all old news.

▪18▪

When I was little, I used to play for hours with plastic soldiers. I'd set them up everywhere in my room — on the floor, on my chest of drawers, my nightstand. I'd have them in lines of two and three and four. Once they were all set up, I'd smash them here, there, and everywhere. I was in complete control. Every little plastic man did exactly what I wanted.

I think that's what I wanted from Josh those days. I wanted him to be like one of my plastic soldiers. I wanted him to do what I wanted.

I had it all worked out. I'd give him a week to get over the battering he'd taken from O'Dea. Then he'd be ready for baseball. We'd throw at the Community Center after school and hang out together at night. It would be just like summer, only better, because I'd be better. My ankle felt good; I had more stamina; and it seemed like my foot speed was picking up, though it's hard to know about that unless somebody times you.

The problem was I couldn't get him to play ball. After school he wanted to hang around in his room and talk football. O'Dea was cruising through the state tournament, and every one of their victories ate at him. "That should be us playing," he'd say, as he looked at the newspaper. "That should be me out there." Even after O'Dea crushed Bellingham for the state title, he still wouldn't do anything.

"Forget football," I kept telling him. "It's time to start thinking about baseball."

113

"Pretty soon," he'd answer. "Pretty soon."

Right before the Christmas break, my grades came in the mail. I'd done better than ever before, all A's and B + 's. My parents were happy, especially with the B + in chemistry. "We know that's a hard class," my mom said, and I was glad she realized it had been tougher to earn than my A in art. Those grades somehow got me even more pumped up to play baseball. I felt that I was on a roll, and I didn't want to lose my momentum.

That night Josh and I took the bus down to the waterfront and walked around, doing nothing. After a while we were both hungry, so we got some fish and chips at Ivar's, sat outside under their heaters, and looked at the ferries moving across the Puget Sound.

"How about if we start throwing the ball around once vacation starts?" I asked.

He shook his head. "Can't do it. We're going to L.A. to see my brother over Christmas." He must have seen the disappointment in my face. "Don't blame me, Ryan. It's not my idea."

I bit into a piece of fish, swallowed.

"Look," he said, "as soon as I get back, we'll start throwing the ball around. Absolutely the first thing."

"Is that a promise?" I asked.

"It's a promise."

I used to love Christmas, especially all the little things that come with it. I was the one who cracked the eggs, measured the butter and flour, stirred up the batter for the cookies. I passed the strings of outdoor lights up to my father on the ladder. I hung the fancy ornaments on the tree; I lit the candles at Christmas dinner.

But I'm seventeen years old now, and the thrill is gone from that stuff, though my parents don't seem to realize it. As Christmas neared, I heard the same old phrases. "Ryan, you can lick the bowl if you want!" "Ryan, you can put the angel on top of the tree!" "Ryan, I'll pass the lights up to you and you can hang them!" It's kind of sad, the way they think that I'm still ten. But it's irritating too, and it puts me in a foul mood.

My grandfather Kevin always comes a couple of days before Christmas and stays until New Year's Day. He's my father's father, and he's okay. Other than his fingers, which are gnarled and arthritic, he still looks good. He stands straight and tall; his hair is white and shiny and full; he swims every day. He doesn't go on and on about how hard things were when he grew up. In fact, the only thing I don't like about him is that he gets my bed and I have to sleep downstairs on the sofa.

For years Grandpa Kevin has given me a fair chunk of money for Christmas. There's always been a note with it: "For your college education." It's nice of him and all, but since I've never been all that sure about going to college, I would have liked to have spent at least some of it right then.

I figured on money again, but Christmas morning there was a big box under the tree marked: "For Ryan, from Grandpa Kevin." Inside were a catcher's mitt, chest protector, mask, shin guards.

"Your dad says you're trying out this year," Grandpa Kevin said as I stared, open-mouthed, at the unexpected gifts. "You probably don't know it, but I used to catch. I was pretty good, too. If you want, I'll show you a few things later on."

I was plenty glad to get the gear. It was high quality stuff, all name brands, the best. And I let him know that I appreciated the gifts. But listening to tips from a seventy-year-old ex–ball player was not something I wanted to do. "Sure," I said, halfheartedly. "That'd be great. Later on we'll have to do it."

I hoped he wouldn't bring it up again, but after we'd eaten breakfast, he asked again. "Maybe this afternoon, Grandpa," I said. "I'm pretty full right now."

I thought I was being clever, but he smiled in a way that let me know I wasn't fooling him. "Well, it was just an idea."

That was it. No lecture on how much I could learn if I'd only listen. As I said, he's okay.

Around two o'clock that afternoon I thought: *Why not?* I was bored and there was nothing else to do. Playing ball with Grandpa Kevin might be better than nothing, and it would kill the guilt. So I went upstairs and tapped on my own door. "Grandpa, you still want to show me some stuff?"

His face lit up.

We went to the backyard. He turned a garbage can onto its side so that the open end faced across the yard. On the other side of the yard, as far away as possible, he laid down an old doormat.

"This is home base," he said, "and that garbage can is second. I'll pitch a ball to you. You pretend somebody is stealing. I want to see you throw the base runner out."

"It's not nearly far enough," I protested. "You can't tell anything about my arm from a throw that short."

"I'm not interested in your arm strength. I can't do anything about that anyway. I want to see your form."

I crouched down. He tossed me the ball. Actually that's not fair. He threw it to me with more steam than I expected. I caught it, stood, and threw to the garbage can: a strike that rattled around inside the metal. I thought he'd be impressed, but when I looked at him he was shaking his head.

"What was wrong with that?" I asked. "It was right on the money."

"The throw was accurate and strong, sure. But my God, Ryan, even I might have made it to second by the time you got rid of the ball. A speedster would have gone in standing up."

I didn't like what he was saying. And I didn't like the way he was saying it, either. But there are times when people talk and you just know they know what they're talking about. That's how it was with Grandpa Kevin. I swallowed my pride.

"How does a catcher throw?"

"You want me to show you?"

"Yeah. I do."

He reworked everything about my motion. "As soon as a base runner reaches first, you start preparing to throw him out at second. You dig your toes into the dirt a little deeper so you can come out of your crouch faster. And you watch him out of the corner of your eye.

"If he goes, you're starting your throw even as you're catching the ball. You swing your mitt and your right hand up toward your right shoulder, taking the ball out as you do it. Once the ball is in your right hand, extend your left arm forward and cock your right wrist at your ear. No farther back than that, or you won't get rid of the ball in time. As you step toward second, fire the ball right at the bag."

It wasn't easy to understand what he meant, and after he walked me through it a dozen times, I discovered it wasn't easy to do it. He kept telling me I had to be quicker, but I felt all tied up in the gear — the mask, chest protector, shin guards.

It took three cold, drizzly afternoons before I was even okay with the throwing motion. Then he had me work on coming out of my crouch differently. "You don't want to come straight up," he said. "You want to come forward and up. That way you get clear of the hitter, you've got a better look at the bag, and you've got a foot or two less distance to throw. Those two feet can be the difference between nailing a runner and having him slide in under the tag."

When he wasn't teaching me, we talked baseball. I'd ask him some simple question like "Did you ever see Johnny Bench?" and he'd describe games in a way I'd never heard them described before — the way a catcher would see them. As he talked, I could imagine the whole field. He told me how a good catcher positions fielders based on the stuff his pitcher has, and that proper positioning sometimes changes from inning to inning, even pitch to pitch. The more he talked, the more I wanted to hear. The cat-and-mouse game between pitcher and hitter — suddenly I could see myself controlling that, deciding when to call for the curve or the slider, when to come with the big heat or the change.

I'd thought that being a catcher was like eating leftovers, something I was going to do because there was no other choice. But Grandpa Kevin changed that.

"Messing up your ankle might be the best thing you ever did," he said the morning he left.

"How did you figure?" I asked.

He smiled. "Well, otherwise you would never have become a catcher."

It was a crazy thing to say. Crazier still, I believed him.

▪ 20 ▪

Grandpa Kevin left early New Year's morning. I was sorry to see him go. He'd connected me with baseball again, and I'd have gladly given up my room for as long as he'd wanted it to keep that connection.

That was a strange day. The sun was out, which

doesn't happen much in January. But instead of getting warmer, the air grew colder every hour. The sky was strange too. The clouds were high and a different, whiter color than usual.

"It's going to snow," my dad said.

My mom groaned. "Don't say that."

Seattle has lots of hills and no snowplows. It doesn't snow often here, but when it does, even if it's only an inch or two, the whole city shuts down.

"You wait," he said.

My father spent New Year's Day watching bowl games on television. He kept asking me to join him, but I couldn't watch for long. I'd see some quarterback get massacred and I'd think about Josh, and it just wasn't fun. I went out to the yard and practiced throwing the way Grandpa Kevin had shown me, but even that didn't work. You can only do so much alone.

We ate dinner. The Fiesta Bowl game was for the national championship. "You're going to watch that with me, aren't you?" my dad said. He had a worried look in his eyes, like I was sick or something, so I sat down with him and watched it, or at least pretended to watch it. When the game ended, I was glad to escape to my room. I turned on my radio and flipped through magazines. It was after midnight when I flicked off the light.

I don't remember going to sleep. I only remember waking up and noticing right away that my room was brighter than it should have been.

I went to the window, and there it was. Snow. Big soft flakes floating down. I could see them in the streetlights, millions and millions of snowflakes, swirling downward.

I stood, mesmerized, and watched as a fine layer of white formed on top of the lawn and the street. Still more snow came. For a while I could still see little patches of green or little bits of gray underneath the cars. Finally even the green and gray patches were gone. There wasn't a footprint or a tire track anywhere. All the world was white and clean and beautiful. It could have been the very first day of creation.

I don't know what time it was when I fell back to sleep. Early the next morning there was a tapping on my door. "Ryan," my mother whispered, "are you awake?"

I almost rolled over and covered my head with the pillow. I don't know why I didn't. But for some reason, I answered. "Yeah, I'm awake," I said.

She opened the door a crack. "Josh is downstairs. Shall I tell him to come back later?"

I sat straight up. "No. No," I said. "Tell him I'll be right down."

There was a pause. Then she continued, her voice lower. "Ryan, he said for you to bring your catcher's mitt. But you're not going to play baseball in this, are you?"

I'll never forget that day. What we were doing was crazy. Snow was still falling, and the white baseball got lost in the flurries, got lost against the totally white backdrop. We were so bundled up we could hardly run or throw. Josh shouted things to me about Los Angeles, and I shouted back to him about my grandfather. I only heard about half of what he said and I figure he heard about the same of what I said. The words didn't matter. The snow didn't matter. The cold didn't matter. I was laughing my head off, and so was Josh. We were playing ball together again.

Part Three

▪ 1 ▪

After that we threw every day. Josh was loosey-goosey, trying knucklers and slurves and all sorts of weird pitches. I wished I could have joined in the fun, but I wasn't loosey-goosey at all. Nowhere close. Grandpa Kevin had taught me a lot, but the main thing I'd learned was that I didn't know much about catching.

In the summer, baseball season had been like a bright rainbow off in the sky somewhere, not quite real. But now it was less than two months away, and as much as I wanted it, that's how much I was afraid of it.

Josh noticed. "What's eating you? I thought you wanted to play ball."

"I do."

"So?"

"So, I'm nervous. You know you're going to make the team, but I don't."

He waved that off. "You'll make it. I told you. You've got great hands. Besides, nobody wants to play catcher."

"But what about the other stuff? Defense and giving signs and positioning fielders and backing up and all that. I don't know anything about that. And I haven't swung the bat in five years."

He threw me another knuckler. I tossed it back.

"You won't have any trouble learning," he said. "It's simple. I could teach you if you want."

I leaped at the suggestion. "Would you?"

He threw again. "Sure."

"Well, let's do it then."

"You mean right now?"

"Why not?"

"No reason, I guess." He stared at me. "What do you want to learn first?"

"That's just it, Josh," I said, frustrated. "I don't know. You tell me. What am I doing wrong? What should I do different?"

He thought for a while. "This is a little thing."

"I don't care. Tell me and I'll work on it."

He took off his cap, ran his hand through his hair. "Well, I don't like the way you throw the ball back to me after a pitch."

I didn't get what he was saying.

"Your throws aren't all the same," he explained. "Sometimes I'm reaching up; sometimes I'm rooting around in the dirt. In a game, when I'm in a groove or trying to get in one, I want that ball coming back to me the same way every single time. I want to be able to catch it without thinking about it. All I want to think about is pitching."

He was right. I didn't pay attention to the throw I made to him. I just threw it. I got the ball to him, but my throws were everywhere: high, low, left, right.

So I worked on it. He'd pitch, then hold his glove up, and I'd try to hit it — the same throw every time, the same speed to the same place.

Little by little I got better. Finally he'd hold up his glove and my throw would be on its way. Smack! He'd go back to the mound, pitch again. I'd catch it, fire it back. Smack! Pitch . . . catch . . . throw . . . catch . . . pitch . . . catch . . . throw . . . catch. We had our own rhythm.

Once I had that down, we moved to signs. On television they seem simple enough. One finger means fastball; two fingers means curve; three is the slider; four is the change.

The problem was that after I'd call for a pitch, I'd sometimes forget what pitch I'd called for. Josh would be into his wind-up and I'd be wondering if he was coming with heat or if he was throwing the curve. Even worse were the times when I was certain I'd called for a fastball and he'd throw me a breaking pitch, or the other way around. Everything feels wrong when that happens. It's like when you go to sit down in a chair and some fool has pulled it out from under you.

As the weeks passed we moved on to other parts of the game. On infield pop-ups, it's the catcher who decides what infielder makes the play. Josh explained how to decide based on where the sun was, where the baserunners were, and who was the best fielder. He told me what bases I backed up on ground balls and fly outs. "On throws to home plate from the outfield," he said, "the catcher decides whether to cut them off. If you scream out 'Cut one,' it means you want the infielder to cut the ball off and throw behind the runner at first. *Cut two* means go to second. *Cut three* and the ball goes to third. Don't let a throw come through if you have no play at the plate. You can stop a lot of rallies by cutting the ball and nailing a careless runner."

The last thing we worked on was the throw to second. When he saw my form and my velocity, he let out a low whistle. "That's good," he said. "Really good. You're a natural at that."

I should have told him about Grandpa Kevin, but after feeling like I knew nothing for so many weeks, it felt good having him think of me as a natural for once.

Hitting was the joker in the deck. Whenever I started thinking that I was catching pretty decently, I'd imagine myself whiffing every pitch that came across the plate. So I kept putting off asking Josh to pitch to me. Finally he asked me if I wanted to take some swings.

"Yeah, sure," I said. "I'll bring my bat tomorrow."

"No need. I brought mine today."

He could have made an idiot of me. If he'd changed speeds, thrown me all the pitches he was capable of throwing, I would have swung and missed over and over. That would have destroyed me. I wouldn't have been able to hit anybody.

But he brought me along like you'd bring along a little kid. He started by throwing fat fastballs right down the middle. Over and over he grooved them, and I spanked them around the park. We'd go pick them up, and then he'd groove another dozen to me.

He'd talk as he pitched. "If a pitcher has got control, then go up there swinging. But if he's wild — and most of them will be — then take. Once you get ahead in the count, look for your pitch in your zone."

Eventually we simulated game situations. He'd tell me there was a runner on second with nobody out, and that my job was to hit the ball to the right side and move the runner up. Then he'd pitch, and I'd take my hacks at hitting grounders toward second base.

"You got to get used to failing," he said. "Because you're going to make more outs than hits. When I'm pitching, the guys that scare me are the guys who shrug off a strikeout or two or three. If I fan a guy and see him brooding on the bench or in the field, then I know I've got him for the whole game. But if he's still got his head up, then I've got my work cut out for me."

I'd been a solid hitter in Little League, and with practice my swing came back. I was spraying line drives all around the park. I wanted to feel good about what I'd accomplished, but I knew Josh was babying me along, and that no other pitcher would.

"Look," I said one day when he was about to start throwing, "maybe you should pitch me tougher. Nobody is going to throw fat fastballs and hanging curves to me."

He shook his head. "You're dead wrong about that. You're going to see lots of fat fastballs and hanging curves. They're the pitches you're going to hit."

I thought about that. "But what happens when I meet a really good pitcher, a pitcher like you?"

A mocking smile crossed his face. "Then you strike out."

It was my turn to smile. "Thanks," I said. "Thanks a lot."

He shrugged. "Just telling you the truth."

• 2 •

I knew he hadn't forgotten about Monica Roby, any more than she'd forgotten about him. But I did think that they'd reached a sort of truce. If she spoke in class, he didn't laugh or talk or sneer. On her part, she'd put out another issue of the *Viper*. I went through it word by word, expecting some new dig at Josh, but there was nothing there.

Then came the football scholarship fiasco.

The first week of February Josh started getting real tense. His eyes were always in the distance, and he hardly spoke. When he did talk, it was always the same. "Three schools are looking at me," he said again and again, "but it all depends on what other guys do." Then he'd bite his lip. "If we'd made the state tournament, if they could have seen me against the best, I'd have a lock on it."

Letter-of-intent day came and his phone didn't ring. And it didn't ring the next day either. Not Washington

State, not San Jose State, not Nevada-Reno. Sunday afternoon we were back at the diamonds throwing the ball. I could feel his anger in the speed of his fastball. "The coach at San Jose says I can walk on," he told me between pitches, "and that if I make the team he'll give me a scholarship next year."

"That's something, isn't it?" I answered. "Lots of walk-ons end up being starters."

"I'll do it if I have to." Then he looked at the baseball he had in his hand. "But if I pitch like I *can* pitch, I'm not going to have to."

All through the lunch period on Monday, a steady stream of guys came up and asked if he'd gotten a scholarship. Time after time he explained he hadn't. "You want to eat outside?" I asked after he'd gone through it for about the sixth time.

"Why should I?" he said, his voice challenging.

I shrugged. "I thought you might be sick of questions."

"They can ask whatever they want. I don't care."

But when yet another guy came up, Josh picked up his tray and walked out of the cafeteria. I let him go.

You read in the newspaper how big stars complain they don't have any privacy, but you don't feel sorry for them. You think: I'd trade privacy for fame any day. But I felt for Josh that day. It was as though he had an open wound, and everybody kept coming up to look at it.

Then came the final insult. Just before the dismissal bell the intercom crackled, and Mr. Haskin came on. His voice was excited, bubbling with pride. "For the first time in four years, Crown Hill High School can count a

National Merit Scholar among its students. Congratulations to Monica Roby on her great achievement. Hard work and study do pay off!"

▪ 3 ▪

Josh didn't say anything about Monica. Not while we were throwing that afternoon, not afterwards when we went to the Ballard Bakery and ate scones and drank orange juice. But I knew it was working on his mind. His bitterness came out the next day in English.

We'd just finished reading *The Pearl*. It's a decent book about this dirt-poor pearl diver, Kino, who lives in a fishing village somewhere in Central America. One day Kino finds this huge black pearl. But when he goes to sell it, the pearl buyers in town don't offer him much. They tell him the pearl is too big, that its color is too strange, that nobody wants it.

Kino is sure they're trying to cheat him, so he refuses to sell. When word gets out that he's still got the pearl, everything falls apart. People try to rob him. They burn his house down and wreck his boat.

His wife, Juana, blames the disasters on the pearl. She snatches it from Kino and runs toward the ocean to chuck it back. Kino chases her down, slaps her, and takes the pearl back.

He decides his only chance is to take his family to a big city and sell the pearl there. So one night they sneak out of town. But on the road more robbers attack. Kino kills them, but in the gunfight they kill his baby. He's so depressed by his son's death that he drags himself back to his village and throws his perfect pearl into the ocean.

I felt for the guy. It seemed like he did everything right, but that everything turned out wrong. Monica saw it differently. "He says he loves his wife and his son," she said during the class discussion, "that he's doing it all for them. But look what happens. He beats up his wife and he gets his baby killed. There's true love! All he really cares about is his silly male pride."

"Anybody else have anything to say?" Ms. Hurley said. "Somebody must have sympathy for Kino."

Probably lots of kids did, but Monica was worked up and no one wanted to tangle with her.

Then, out of nowhere, came Josh's voice: "It's not silly to want to keep your self-respect."

Monica didn't give him a second. "Self-respect?" she retorted in disbelief. "How can a man who beats his wife have any self-respect?"

Josh leaned forward. "He doesn't beat her. He slaps her that one time when she's about to throw the pearl away. He can't let her do it."

"Oh, I like that," she said scornfully. "He can't let her throw the pearl back. Oh no. He beats her when she tries. But it's perfectly okay for him to throw it back. Very logical."

"It *is* logical," Josh said. "It's *his* pearl, not hers. What happens to it has got to be up to him. He can't let her throw it away. Not and still be a man."

"But he can slap his wife around and still be a man. Is that what you're saying?"

Kids groaned. "It's just a book, Monica," someone said.

Monica didn't back down. She stared at Josh. "I want an answer. Is it okay for a man to slap his wife around?"

Josh glared at her. "He had to get the pearl back, no matter what it took."

"Even if it meant hitting her?"

"Since that was the only way, then yes."

Monica looked to the ceiling, her eyes rolling up as if he'd said the stupidest thing she'd ever heard in her life. "That is such a jock mentality," she said. Then she looked right at Josh. "You just don't get it, do you?"

"All right, Monica," Ms. Hurley said, "that's —"

Before she could finish, Josh interrupted, his finger jabbing the air. "Don't you tell me I don't get it. You're the one who doesn't get —"

Ms. Hurley clapped her hands. "That's enough out of both of you." Her voice was commanding as she looked from Josh to Monica. Both of them were furious, glaring at one another. Ms. Hurley kept staring at them as she spoke to us. "You can have a study period for the last ten minutes of class today. And I mean study. No talking at all."

I didn't talk to Josh about what had happened. I didn't know what to say. But the next day, when Ms. Hurley bravely took up the discussion right where she'd stopped it, I felt my hands go cold. Nothing happened, though.

Josh barely paid attention, and Monica had the field to herself.

The whole incident reminded me of something that occurred on a camping trip I'd once taken with my father to Mink Lake. It had been a gray day, and as night fell the sky clouded over. It was so dark we couldn't see the water, though we were only about twenty feet from it. As the hours passed, the air grew thicker and thicker. Then, around midnight, great bolts of lightning lit up the sky. We could see the whole lake more clearly than we'd ever seen it in the daylight. The storm lasted about ten minutes, and then suddenly it was over, as if it had never been.

That's how their argument was. While it was going on, you could see the hostility between those two. But once it ended, everything seemed normal again.

▪ 4 ▪

It's funny how things work. When tryouts were two weeks off, I was chafing at the bit, dying to get out there on the field and show my stuff. I was cocky, sure I'd be both a good catcher and a good hitter.

But the night before the tryout, I was a total mess. All the old fears came back: I wasn't fast enough; I wouldn't be able to hit. Ten times that night I decided that I wouldn't try out at all.

What got me onto the field was knowing Josh would

be there. I pictured the two of us playing catch, the ball going back and forth, back and forth — just like at the Community Center.

But when it came to it, the tryout was a lot different. As soon as he stepped inside the locker room, Josh was surrounded by Santos and Ruben and Wilsey and other guys from the football team. They were patting him on the back, telling him how great it was that he was trying out and how good the team was going to be. Josh ate it up. He was the guy with the golden arm, and they all knew it. I was nobody.

I dressed quickly and wandered out onto the grass. A group had formed around Josh. Other guys stood together with their friends. I was the only player standing by himself.

It was a relief when Coach Wheatley, a silver-haired guy who didn't teach at Crown Hill, blew his whistle and called us to him. "Twenty-five jumping jacks!" he barked. "Fifty sit-ups!" "Twenty pushups!"

Once we'd all broken a sweat, Wheatley laid some orange traffic cones on the outfield grass. "All right," he shouted. "Time for windsprints. Form groups of six. Come on! Get a move on!"

Every day when I'd worked, I'd told myself that my goal was to get myself to where I had average speed. But as my group worked its way to the start line, average wasn't on my mind. I wanted to win. I wanted to cross that finish line first.

"Ready . . . go!"

I almost slipped on my first step, but I quickly regained

my balance, churned my legs, and worked my arms. I passed one guy, and then another. Maybe I caught another guy, but that was it. At the finish line I was right in the middle of the pack — either third or fourth.

Josh gave me the thumbs up sign, like I'd really accomplished something. And since I hadn't come in last, I guess I had. But it's hard to celebrate being mediocre.

Wheatley didn't let us rest. It was back to the end of the line for more windsprints, more finishes right in the middle of the pack.

Mr. Cliff, an assistant coach with a bushy mustache and long straggly hair, was checking with guys in between races, asking questions and writing stuff down. Finally, he came over to me. "What's your name?"

I told him.

He looked over his roster. "It says here you're a senior, but you've never played before. How come?"

"I played Little League," I said. "Center field. Then I hurt my ankle and kind of quit."

"So what made you kind of 'unquit'?" he asked.

"I thought I might be able to catch."

His eyebrows went up. "Have you ever caught before?"

"Not on a team," I said, "but I've caught some."

"We've got our first-string catcher returning from last year's team," he said. "And another guy who can back him up. Besides, being a catcher is a lot harder than you might think."

"All I want is a chance," I said. "If I'm no good you can cut me."

He snorted. "Don't worry about that. If you're no good we *will* cut you." Then he moved to another player.

A whistle blew. Coach Wheatley emptied a ball bag onto the ground. "Grab your gloves, find a partner and play some catch. Two lines. One group against the fence, the other group about twenty paces away. Let's go! Move it!"

Around me everyone was in motion, running to their equipment bags for their gloves, pairing up. I stood, almost paralyzed. I might have walked off the field right then if Josh hadn't come up.

"Get your stuff, Ryan," he said.

We warmed up for about ten minutes. With each throw and catch my heartbeat slowed, the fear subsided. The whistle blew again. I looked to Wheatley. "Pitchers go with Coach Cliff. The rest of you stay here."

"Good luck," Josh said.

Coach Wheatley pointed to home plate. "If you're willing to catch," he said, "get behind the plate. Otherwise spread out around the infield."

I followed Wheatley toward the backstop, and so did two other guys. One of them was Chris Selin. I knew he'd be there. He was a senior, a three-year letterman, and a two-year starter. The other guy was Garrett Curtis, the sophomore from the football team who ran back kicks. "I can play third and first, too," Curtis said to Wheatley, "and a little outfield."

"How about you?" Wheatley asked, turning to me. "You play anywhere else?"

I shook my head. "Just catcher," I said.

He frowned, then made a note on his clipboard.

Wheatley banged grounders to the infielders. We took turns handling their throws back. Then he had us field bunts, run down pop-ups, make the throw to second, hit. My throws were pretty good, but both Selin and Curtis had more range on the pop-ups, more quickness fielding the bunts. During batting practice Curtis blasted two balls over the fence and Selin blistered line drives to all fields. I hit a couple of hard grounders back up the middle, but the rest were pop-ups and lazy flies. Coach Wheatley constantly wrote notes on his clipboard. I knew what the words next to my name said without even looking at them: *Mediocre runner. Mediocre fielder. Mediocre hitter.* Finally the whistle blew. "That does it for today. See you tomorrow, gentlemen."

I went to the locker room, changed without showering, and slipped out a side door. Josh called to me as I left, but I pretended I didn't hear him.

The locker room exit opened to a hallway parallel to the three-hundred wing. I walked past empty classroom after empty classroom, then turned and took the shortcut up the hill.

As I neared the music portable at the top, I heard someone practicing the piano. The music was so sunny, so quick and playful, that it was as if whoever was playing was making fun of me. They had a ton of talent, and I had none.

Finally I was there, right outside the portable. Instead of walking by, I stopped and peered through the one window. The room was dark, but I could make out a girl

139

at the piano, her hands gliding back and forth effortlessly. She turned her head slightly and I recognized her.

Monica Roby.

I stepped back and away from the window. I laughed, a disgusted laugh. It *would* be Monica.

That night Josh called. "Why did you disappear?"

I played dumb. "What do you mean?"

"You just took off after practice. I called out to you. Didn't you hear me?"

"No, I didn't."

"Anyway, how did it go for you?"

"Okay," I said. "How about with you?"

"Really good," he said, his voice picking up. "Coach Cliff knew who I was and all, and that made it easier. He didn't want me to throw hard, but I cut loose a couple of times just to show him what I had."

"And?"

Josh laughed. "Coach Cliff's mouth fell open. After one fastball he took his hand out of the mitt and shook it. I'll be starting opening day."

We talked a little longer, and then I told him I had some chemistry homework. That was true, but after I hung up I didn't do it. Instead I lay back and looked at the ceiling.

I'd been waiting for seven months. Planning for seven months. But it had all been a dream, a stupid kid's dream. I had as much chance of making the team as I had of sitting down at the piano and playing Mozart.

▪ 5 ▪

The second day of tryouts was a repeat of day one. Running, throwing, catching, hitting. The clipboard was always there in Wheatley's hand, and I knew the paper on it was filling up with the little marks that were killing my chance to make the team.

I couldn't slip away from Josh again, so I went through the regular locker room routine and then walked home with him.

"How did you do?" he asked once we got outside.

I decided to come clean. "Look," I said, "this was always a long shot for me. I don't regret anything, and I'll catch for you any time you want. But I'm not going to make the team. Selin is better than I am. And Curtis can play third base and first and fill in behind the plate whenever they need him. If I was a sophomore or a junior, maybe I'd have a chance. But they don't need me this year, and I won't be here next. I'm going to get cut."

He didn't argue, and I'm glad he didn't. You want the truth from your friends, not pie-in-the-sky stuff. We walked all the way to our houses in silence. Then, just before we split up, he stopped. "There may still be a way."

"How?"

He bit his lip. "I'd tell you, but it's got a better chance of working if you don't know."

I was irritated. "What's that supposed to mean?"

"Forget I mentioned it," he said, and he was up his porch steps and into his house.

141

But I couldn't forget it. I didn't like his air of secrecy. I couldn't figure what he had planned — whether he was going to go in and plead my case to Coach Wheatley, or whether he'd concocted some way to cheat that I couldn't even imagine. Either way, I wanted no part of it. I'd make the team, or not make it, entirely on my own.

The next day was the final day of tryouts. As Josh and I warmed up together, I told him I wanted things on the up-and-up. "Don't worry," he said. "Just relax and play. Everything is going to work out."

Before I could ask him how, Wheatley blew his whistle and Josh went off with Coach Cliff and the other pitchers.

I had batting practice first thing. I hit the ball pretty well, and to all fields, by far my best effort in the cage. But Selin and Curtis hit the ball well too. And with the other stuff — fielding the bunts and the pop-ups, running the windsprints — they had me. Even my throw down to second, which I'd thought was so good, was only slightly better than their efforts. I wondered if Wheatley even noticed.

With half an hour left in practice, Coach Cliff came walking toward the main diamond, Josh and David Reule and the other pitchers trailing behind him.

Coach Wheatley looked up, surprised. As the two coaches huddled, Josh sidled up next to me. "So far, so good," he said, a light in his eyes.

"What's the deal?" I asked, annoyed.

"You'll see."

A minute later we were paired off. Selin caught Josh;

Curtis caught Reule; and I caught the third pitcher, Randy Wilkerson. Wheatley took his pen out, and lots of little marks were being tallied up on the clipboard.

Right away Chris Selin had trouble handling Josh. About every fourth ball Josh threw got by. "Get in front of those," Wheatley called to Selin.

"I'm trying to," Selin said. "His ball just moves."

Suddenly I understood what Josh was doing.

Josh's next pitch got by Selin too. Coach Wheatley pointed to Selin and Curtis. "You two, switch."

Curtis handled Josh better at first, but then one ball got by him, then another, and another. Wheatley moved directly behind Curtis. "That's a slider you're throwing," he called out to Josh. "And a pretty good one."

"Is it?" Josh answered, acting dumb.

The next pitch got by Curtis. As he trotted off to retrieve it, Josh motioned toward me. "How about if I throw to Ryan a little," he said. "Maybe he could handle my stuff better."

Wheatley shrugged. "Sure. Why not? Let's see what Ryan can do."

So Curtis and I switched. And with both Coach Cliff and Coach Wheatley watching, Josh fired slider after slider at me. He came at me with his best stuff — the stuff that was eating up Curtis and Selin.

Nothing got by.

After practice, as we headed to the locker room, Josh wrapped his arm around me and gave me a shake. "You did it, big guy!" he said. "You showed them you can catch."

My heart was racing and a big grin was trying to cover my face. I wasn't sure I'd made the team, but I had a chance. And it had been fair and square, on the field.

"Thanks for the help," I said. "Thanks a lot."

He smiled. "Don't thank me. I didn't do anything. I just threw the ball. You're the one who caught it."

I stopped him there. "I don't mean just today. I mean all the days. I'd never have gotten anywhere without your help, and I know it."

He punched me on the shoulder. "I didn't do it for you. I did it for myself. A pitcher needs a good catcher."

I slept that night. I wasn't confident, or even close to being confident. But tryouts were over. Whatever was going to happen was going to happen.

I wasn't calm in the morning, though. I raced through my breakfast. I was at school so early I had to wait for them to open up the main doors. I hustled down to the gym. Outside the main entrance is the P.E. bulletin board.

I spotted the list from about ten yards: "Varsity Baseball Team." It was neatly typed. I ran my finger down the list. Josh was there, of course, and so were Garrett Curtis and Chris Selin. And then, at the very bottom of the list, was my name.

Ryan Ward.

▪ 6 ▪

They say you should never be satisfied with what you've got, that you should always be trying for more. And since everybody says it, I suppose it's true. But the fact is I *was* satisfied. When I came back out after reading my name at the bottom of the roster, the sun was shining, and I felt like it was shining just for me.

I didn't care that at our first practices Coach Wheatley stuck me out along the right field line and had me protect the pitchers and catchers who were warming up during batting practice. I was happy to field the occasional stray grounder or line drive. Crown Hill's colors are red and black, and the baseball uniform has a Viking ship on the sleeve. It's a sharp-looking uniform, and I was going to get one with my name sewn on the back. That's all that mattered.

After one of those early practices, Josh and I came out of the locker room together. The sky was a reddish pink and a blazing sun was setting over the Olympic Mountains. In the distance I heard Monica playing the piano. "Isn't that incredible?" I said, without thinking.

Josh looked at me, surprised. "You like classical stuff?"

I shook my head. "Not really. It's just that for a second it sounded really good."

We walked down the hallway. The air vibrated with music. It raced down the hall the same way Monica's hands must have been racing over the keyboard.

"I wonder who's playing?" Josh said as we turned up the hill toward the portable.

"Who cares?" I answered, trying to lead him past it.

"I want to see. I didn't know anybody in this school was any good at anything." He grinned. "Besides me, of course."

He leaned down and peered in the window just as I had. Then he pulled back, as though he'd put his hand on a red hot iron. "It's Monica Roby," he said, disbelief on his face. "Is there anything she doesn't do?"

I grabbed him by the elbow and pulled him from the window. "She doesn't play baseball," I said, "so don't worry about her."

▪ 7 ▪

By a weird fluke of scheduling, we opened the season against O'Dea, making it one of the biggest games of the season. Josh was pumped for a bunch of different reasons. They were the defending league champions, so beating them would get us off on the right foot. But it was personal too. Lots of football players would be on the baseball team. He remembered what they had done to him, the punishment they'd laid on him. All week he talked about evening the score.

My father drove me to Woodland Park. In the car he talked about how proud he was of me, how he admired my spirit. I know he was trying to connect with me, but I was too nervous to listen closely, let alone answer.

Coach Wheatley gave us a pep talk I don't remember at all. Then I stretched, ran a little, did some infield practice, and got a few batting practice cuts. The next thing I knew the umpire was shouting: "Play ball!" Josh and the other starters — including Curtis, whose big bat had won him the third-base job — took their places on the diamond, and I headed to the bench.

Right then I felt totally deserted. There were other guys not playing, of course. Darren Smith and Kolas Chang and Mike Nelson. David Reule, our number two starter. Carlos Hernandes, the designated hitter. But we didn't talk. We spread out on the bench, each of us feeling there was something wrong with us, each of us trying to be invisible, each of us aching to play.

It was better once the game started. O'Dea's leadoff guy was thin as a pencil and fast as lightning. He showed bunt on the first pitch, but Josh burned a fastball over the heart of the plate. Strike two was another fastball on the outside corner. With the guy leaning out over the plate a little, Josh came back inside with still another fastball. The batter jumped out of the way as if it was close to hitting him, but Selin didn't have to move his mitt. "Strike three!" the ump hollered.

"That's the way to pitch!" Wheatley shouted.

I cheered, and so did all the other guys on the bench. But once the cheer ended, we lapsed back into silence. There's nothing much to do on the bench.

O'Dea's number two guy grounded out to third,

147

bringing up the three hitter, Number Forty. He looked familiar, but I couldn't figure how I could know him. Then it came to me: the number, the build — he was the linebacker who had sacked Josh so many times in the football game.

I looked out at Josh's face, and I knew he knew it too. He got a first pitch strike on a curve. Then he came in with a hard fastball, high and tight, that put Forty down in the dirt. The pitch would have beaned him if he'd been a tenth of a second slower. Forty stood, dusted himself off, then glared out at Josh.

It wasn't just show, either. The guy was tough. Josh came back with another curve on the outside part of the plate. You figure that after a fastball up and in, the batter is not going to be leaning out over the plate any time too soon. But Forty went out and got that ball, rifling a shot down the first base line that Dillon Combs caught without moving an inch. He was out, but Josh hadn't fooled him.

The starters clattered into the dugout. Josh sat down by himself at the end of the bench. I started toward him, but he put a towel over his head and closed himself off.

Around me all the other guys seemed to have somebody to talk to. I felt like a stranger with nothing to say and no one to say it to. I looked back to where I'd been and saw Ruben sitting there. I leaned against the Cyclone fence, twining my fingers through it, and stared out to the field.

The O'Dea pitcher was tight, and he walked Van Tassel on four pitches. Once he threw his first strike he settled down, and Curtis, Richardson, and Bayne went down easily. The way the O'Dea infielders made the putouts told you they were good. The third baseman bare-handed Curtis's dribbler and threw a strike on the run, and the shortstop was smooth as silk on Combs's two-hopper. There was no way we were going to blow them out — not with the pitching and fielding they had.

In the second inning I watched Selin, watched the way he called the game. He was moving Josh's pitches in and out, changing speeds. But there was something not quite right, something missing. It wasn't until the third that I figured it out: no sliders.

Selin had handled the slider better in practice, but he wasn't calling for it in the game. Not with no strikes, not with two strikes. It was lack of confidence, and it was pride too. You don't want balls getting by you when you're catching, especially with people watching. So he kept Josh throwing fastballs and curves.

It didn't matter as long as Josh was getting everybody out, but in the fourth, Josh lost the plate. He walked the first guy on five pitches, then hit the number two batter. That brought up Number Forty again, this time with a chance to do some serious damage.

Selin called time and went out to the mound to go over strategy. I knew what I would have done, how I'd have pitched Forty. I'd have started him out with the slider to get him thinking. Then I would have busted a fastball in on his hands, wasted a curve outside, and polished him off with another slider. Change speeds; change locations; keep him off balance.

But that's not what Selin did. He called for heat, heat, and more heat. Josh blew the first fastball right past Forty. And he got a strike on the second fastball, too. Only on that one, Forty got a piece of it and sent a foul ball straight back into the screen.

You can tell a lot from foul balls. If they're hit down the right or left field lines, then the pitcher has got the hitter's timing off, and he's in control. But a foul ball straight back — that means trouble. The hitter has the pitch timed, and the pitcher had better do something different — and do it quick.

I stood, leaned against the fence. "The slider," I whispered. "Call for the slider." But Selin wanted another fastball, and Josh would never shake off the heater. Forty was right on it, and I thought he'd driven the ball all the way to Green Lake, but he was just under it. Still, the ball carried to the warning track in straightaway center before Andy Bayne hauled it in. Both runners tagged and moved up a base, but at least there was one out.

Wheatley held up four fingers, so Josh walked the cleanup hitter intentionally to load the bases. Everybody was up now — O'Dea fans and Crown Hill fans — cheering and screaming.

Josh peered in, shook off one sign, then another, and another. Finally Wheatley called time and trotted out to the mound.

Even from the bench you could tell that Josh and Selin were furious with one another. They wouldn't look at each other, and Wheatley kept swiveling his head back and forth, first talking to one and then to the other. Finally he returned to the bench.

The next pitch was the first slider Josh had thrown all day, and it was a dandy. The batter waved at it as it broke, but the ball got by Selin and rolled all the way to the backstop. The runner on third scored easily, and the other two runners moved up. Wheatley kicked at the Cyclone fence, then looked down the bench toward me.

Josh's next pitch was a fastball right down the pike. The O'Dea hitter sent a shot toward right field that looked like a clean base hit. But Jesse Van Tassel went way up to spear it. The ball stuck in the webbing of his glove like a scoop of vanilla ice cream on a cone. The runner on second had taken off for third, certain the ball was headed up the alley for extra bases. Van Tassel trotted over to the bag to double him up. They'd taken the lead, but we were out of the inning.

The score was still 1–0 heading to the bottom of the sixth. Carlos Hernandes worked a leadoff walk, but our next two guys went down easily — a lazy fly to center and a pop-up to the first baseman. With two down, Bethel Santos ripped the first pitch he saw right back up the middle for a single, moving Hernandes to third. "We had something going at last."

Santos had decent speed, but the O'Dea pitcher acted like he was Rickey Henderson. He should have concentrated on Brandon Ruben, who was batting, but he kept throwing over to first, trying to keep Santos close. When he finally did come to the plate, he served up a fastball belt-high right over the heart of the plate. Ruben was a little late with his swing, but he caught the ball solid and sent a line drive down the right field line. It landed fair by about a foot and kicked into the corner.

Hernandes scored the tying run easily. As Santos flew around second, Wheatley, coaching at third, pinwheeled his arm sending him home. O'Dea should have had him, because the right fielder got the ball cleanly and made a good throw. But the relay from the second baseman was way up the line. Santos slid in safely, and we had the lead.

I'd hardly finished cheering when I heard Wheatley. "You're done for today, Selin. Get your gear on, Ward. You're catching the last inning."

I stared at him, unsure if I'd heard right.

"Come on!" he hollered, clapping his hands. "Get moving!"

My eyes met Selin's. For a second his flashed in anger. But just for a second. "Close them out," he said, as he unbuckled his chest protector. "You can do it."

I'd imagined taking the field as a varsity player for the first time. I pictured myself walking slowly out onto the grass and looking around, like a movie actor, savoring the moment. It didn't work out that way. I still had only one shin guard on when Van Tassel popped up to end the inning. My hands were shaking so much I didn't think I'd ever get the straps right. I waddled onto the field hooking up my chest protector and praying I wouldn't fall flat on my face.

Josh was no help. I sort of smiled at him as I returned his first warm-up, but he looked through me like I wasn't there. So I took a deep breath, crouched, and put on my own game face. *Three outs,* I told myself. *That's all we need. Three outs.*

The number nine hitter led off, a break for us. Even better, he was first-pitch swinging. Josh busted a fastball in on the fists, and he went down on a weak pop to shortstop. It was a gift out, but there weren't going to be any more gifts. The top of the order was up.

O'Dea's leadoff guy was a classic number one. Quick, with a good eye. I figured Wheatley had put me in to catch the slider, so that was the pitch I called. But Josh shook me off and threw another inside fastball instead. The O'Dea hitter laid down a beautiful bunt. Curtis raced in, bare-handed the ball, but fired wildly to first. The ball caromed off the Cyclone fence, and the O'Dea guy didn't stop running until he'd reached third base.

Talk about a tight spot — the tying runner was ninety feet from scoring with the two, three, and four hitters due up.

We had to pull the infield in. Doing that gives the fielders a good shot at cutting down the runner at home on grounders hit right to them. But when you're in close you don't have time to react to balls hit to your right or your left. Easy outs at normal depth become hits.

When the O'Dea hitter saw the infield in, he choked up on the bat. He was going to try to poke a grounder through.

I wanted to save the slider for the strikeout, so I had Josh start him off with an inside fastball. The guy had a good cut, but he was late and fouled it off down the first base line. Next I called for a curve that missed outside.

Then I came back with another fastball, and he fouled it off again.

Now! I thought, putting down three fingers for the slider. *Now!*

Josh nodded, a little smile in his eyes. I knew he was going to break off a wicked one and, with the tying run bluffing down the line at third, I also knew I had to keep the ball from getting by me.

Josh wound and delivered. The guy swung at it like it was a fastball, but it broke late, dancing down and under his bat. I moved with the pitch smooth as could be, catching it off the dirt. "Strike three!"

Two down.

There was no time to relax because Number Forty was stepping up to the plate. He'd had two good at-bats against Josh — the screaming line drive out in the first and the long fly ball that had just missed being a home run. He took about eight vicious practice swings before stepping in.

Josh was tired. I could see it in his face, in the way he leaned forward, his right hand on his knee. There was no way he was going to blow this guy down. I was going to have to outthink him.

Number Forty had watched Josh throw first pitch inside fastballs to three straight hitters. I figured he'd figure he'd get the same thing. So I called for the slider away. I wanted him to see it, even if he didn't swing. He was too comfortable up there, way too comfortable. I wanted him to worry.

And Josh threw a beauty. It was belt high down the

middle, and then it was in the dirt. Forty swung and missed. I blocked it, keeping the ball in front of me and keeping the runner from scoring.

Strike one.

Forty stepped out, pulled on his gloves. I almost smiled, because I knew that slider had hatched some butterflies in his belly. He'd be looking for it again, I decided, so I called for the fastball inside. He started to swing, then tried to check. Too late. "Strike two!" the umpire hollered.

If it had been the second inning, I'd have had Josh waste a pitch. A curveball a foot outside — something like that. But he was too tired to waste any energy. He pinwheeled his arm twice, peered in. I flashed the sign for the slider. He nodded. Looking into his eyes, I knew he was going to throw the best one he had because it was the last one he had. I got ready to move. I couldn't let it get by me.

And there it was, fast and breaking down into the dirt. Forty swung over the top as I slid to my knees to block it. The ball hit against the heel of my mitt and then off my chest protector, rolling out in front of the plate.

Forty took off toward first as I scrambled to my feet and hustled after the ball. I thought my legs would never get there. Finally I picked it up and made a good crisp throw down to first for the game-ending out. The guys swarmed Josh, swarmed him like he'd just won the championship game, not the opening game. And why not? We'd beaten O'Dea! For the first time since who knows when, we'd beaten O'Dea!

Once the celebrating ended, Josh and I sat next to each

155

other on the bench, packing away our stuff. Or rather he was packing up his stuff. I was so excited I just sat.

Coach Wheatley walked by and gave my arm a squeeze. "Nice job out there," he said. "In my book you get the save."

"Thanks," I said, smiling up at him. "Thanks."

"He's right, you know," Josh said when he was gone. "Forty had my fastball timed. The slider was the only pitch I could get him with. Selin would have never called for it, not with a runner at third. You play your cards right and you'll see a lot of action."

"You really think so?" I said, trying not to hope for too much.

Josh zipped up his bag and stood. "I know so."

I didn't answer him. I couldn't. I felt like a tidal wave was welling up inside me. I wanted to sing out for joy, to holler — the way you holler at a rock concert.

Josh started off. "Hey," I called out to him when he was about fifteen feet away. "You feel like doing something tonight. Pool? Or a movie?"

He shook his head. "Can't. I'm taking Missy Radburn out."

I knew Missy from Mrs. Beck's class. She was always popping her gum and turning off the computer in the back of the room so she could use the screen to put on her lipstick. She wouldn't have been my first choice for a date.

"Well, have fun," I said, and right away I felt stupid. I hadn't meant it like that.

But Josh only grinned. "I intend to. I intend to."

▪ 8 ▪

That was a great day, and the next day was almost better. We'd had a big test in chemistry class that I'd studied long and hard for. I thought I'd done pretty well, but when I got it back with a huge "A+" written across the top in red, I was amazed. After class Mr. Woodruff walked down the hall with me. "What are your plans for next year?" he asked.

I told him about Shoreline Community College.

"That's a good school. You can get a start there. But be sure to take hard classes, university-level. Don't sell yourself short."

"What do you mean?" I asked.

"I mean you could go a long way. Have you thought about a career in medicine?"

I laughed out loud. "Me? A doctor?"

"What's funny about that? You've got real skill in the laboratory. Good hands, better hands than I've seen in a long time. And you're strong enough at the academics when you really work at them. It would take work and dedication, but you'd make a good doctor or dentist or veterinarian." He paused. "Anyway, it's something for you to think about."

It was the kind of thing my father and mother had said to me for as long as I can remember. I'd always just blown it off when they'd done it. But coming from Mr. Woodruff, the words sounded different. Or maybe I was different. You work hard at something you're not sure you can do — as I'd worked at baseball — and when

157

you succeed you start thinking that maybe there are other things that had seemed out of reach, but really aren't.

"I'll think about it, Mr. Woodruff," I said, not laughing anymore.

He nodded. "Good."

Toward the end of practice that same afternoon it was Coach Wheatley's turn. I knew something was up when I saw him talking first to Selin and then to Curtis. Finally he called me over.

"I like your defense, Ryan. I like the way you keep the ball in front of you. In fact, I like your defense so much I've decided to move Curtis to third base permanently and make you my only backup at catcher. If we've got a lead late in a game, you're going in. You understand?"

"Yes *sir*," I said, even though I'd never called him "sir" before.

"Good. And one more thing. Chris Selin has a lot of pride, and it's tough to be yanked out of a game. But he's a team player and a class guy. He'll do everything he can to help you. So you listen to him."

That turned out to be true. For the rest of that practice, and during the other practices that week, Selin filled me in on Reule and Wilkerson and Smith, telling me what they liked to throw and when they liked to throw it. "They aren't like Josh," he said, "but they're good pitchers. You handle them right and they'll get you outs."

Thursday afternoon we played Garfield. Through the early innings I sat on the bench next to Josh. He had a big bag of sunflower seeds on the ground in front of him, and he kept stuffing his mouth and then spitting out the shells. He was watching the game, but watching it the way a fan does. He wasn't going to play and he knew it. For me it was different. I'd gotten a taste of playing. And once you get a taste, you want more.

We cruised to an early 5–0 lead. Ruben had two doubles; Selin knocked in three with a bases-loaded single and a sack fly. Our pitcher, David Reule, gave up some pretty solid hits along the way, but Garfield couldn't put anything together, and our defense, especially Curtis at third, made some great plays. It looked like an easy victory.

Then, in the top of the sixth, Reule lost his shutout to a two-out three-run home run. Randy Wilkerson came in to get the final out, but that home run woke up everybody. The game wasn't over.

As we batted in the bottom of the sixth, I kept looking over at Wheatley, hoping he'd tell me to get my gear on. Wilkerson didn't have a slider or any trick pitches, but defense is defense, and that's all that matters late in a game when you've got the lead. Finally our eyes met, and I was glad they did.

"Ward, get your gear on. You're going in."

Josh nudged me. "Good luck," he said.

Catching Wilkerson was entirely different from catching Josh. He had two pitches — a fastball and a curve. He had no clue whether the ball was going inside or outside, high or low.

I wanted to get ahead in the count on the first batter, so I called for a fastball. But the batter was up there swinging, and he took a cut. He must have got the barest piece of the ball, because it almost stuck in my mitt. Almost.

But instead of sticking, it glanced off my mitt and caught the thumb of my flesh hand, tearing the nail clean off. In a flash I was hopping around, shaking my hand out. Blood was flying everywhere.

Coach Wheatley came out and so did the team manager. They sprayed something on it, then bandaged it up. "Can you stay in?" Wheatley asked.

There was no way I was coming out, not even if my thumb was lying on the ground. I answered quickly. "I can play."

He smiled. "That's the spirit."

But my thumb was throbbing. What I wanted was a nice, easy one-two-three inning. I didn't get it.

Wilkerson gave up a solid single to the leadoff hitter. The next Garfield guy popped out to short center. We were lucky on that one, because the pitch looked to me like a batting practice fastball right down the middle.

Wilkerson didn't get lucky with the next pitch, though. It was another fat fastball, and the hitter creamed it into the alley in left center for a run-scoring triple. That cut our lead to 5–4, and put the tying run ninety feet away. It also brought Wheatley out. He took the ball from Wilkerson and motioned to the bullpen for our left-handed reliever, Darren Smith.

Smith was the only freshman on the team. In practice he was fast, but wild, and just looking in his eyes told me how nervous he was. His warm-up pitches were everywhere.

I trotted out. "Just look at my mitt," I said. "Forget about the guy on third. Forget about the batter. Just look at my mitt. You can do it."

I returned behind the plate, crouched, put down one finger, and stuck my mitt belt high in the center of the strike zone. Smith needed a strike, and I was willing to risk that the Garfield guy couldn't hit his fastball even if it was over the middle.

He stretched, checked the runner, came home. The hitter swung, sending a little bloop into short right. Santos started back, then charged. He caught the ball on the dead run.

I peeked toward third. The runner was tagging. They were going to send him.

Santos's throw was a good one. It reached me on one bounce and was just a couple of feet up the first base line. I caught it, then spun back toward the plate. The Garfield guy didn't slide. I dived at him as he lowered his shoulder and hit me the way a linebacker hits a quarterback. The force of the collision bowled me over. I felt my wrist jam into the ground, but somehow I held on to the ball.

"Out!" the umpire yelled, jerking his thumb emphatically toward his ear. "Out!"

▪ 9 ▪

I couldn't practice Friday. My thumb was twice its normal size, my wrist was sore, and I was so stiff from the collision I could barely walk. "You take it easy," Wheatley told me. "We need you for the game tomorrow."

So I didn't participate in the drills. The guys razzed me pretty good, though. Curtis called me Little Jack Horner, and the football players laughed at me for being banged up after one collision. But their razzing only proved I was part of the team, so I didn't care.

Toward the end of practice Selin came over to me. "How do you handle Josh's slider so well?" he asked.

I shrugged. "I don't know. Luck, I guess."

"Come on," he said. "What do you do?"

He was the experienced catcher, so it felt strange to be giving him tips. But that's what I did. I told him about trusting the ball to break, and actually starting to move before it broke. After that we talked about the throw down to second, and I repeated some of the things Grandpa Kevin had told me.

"Thanks a lot," he said, when Wheatley blew the whistle.

My locker was right next to Josh's. As we dressed, he gave me a little nudge. "You better not give away too much," he said softly. "You could end up not playing at all."

"What are you talking about?"

He looked around. "I heard you with Selin. You teach him everything you know, and Wheatley won't need you. You'll end up on the bench for the whole game."

"He's helped me, Josh. He's helped me a lot. And I didn't even have to ask him. Besides, we're all on the same team."

"I know about teams and teamwork," Josh answered, still talking low. "But you've got to look out for yourself. You don't see me showing Reule or Wilkerson or Smith how to throw sliders. And you won't, either."

Walking home we talked about the upcoming games. But the whole time I thought about what he'd said in the locker room. I knew what he was getting at. I'd even thought of it when I'd been giving pointers to Selin. Still, I didn't regret what I'd done.

Over the next two weeks our schedule was soft. The games we played were all against the weakest teams in the league, and they were all routs. Josh beat Cleveland 8–2. The two runs scored on a fly ball Mike Nelson misplayed into a triple in left field in the last of the seventh. Josh was plenty miffed about losing the shutout. He took it out on the last two Cleveland hitters, striking both of them out on wicked sliders they only waved at. His next outing was against Chief Sealth. They barely had enough guys to field a team, and when their pitcher tired, they had to bring in their right fielder and send the pitcher out there. It was like batting practice for us. The final score was 16–1. Josh went five innings and gave up no runs. They scored the run against Wilkerson in the last inning.

The two games that Reule started weren't any closer. We jumped off to good-sized leads in both of them,

and with a lead Reule was tough. He didn't walk anybody; he came right after hitters with his fastball. If
they hit it, chances are our guys in the field could run
it down.

It was great winning those games, great being part of
a team that was 6–0 and ranked tenth in the state, great
catching the last inning or two and getting an at-bat now
and then. When I was with the guys at practice, at games,
and at school I was on top of the world. But when I was
alone I'd find myself thinking about those days back in
Little League, when I'd been a star like Josh, not a late-
inning defensive replacement. I'd wonder how it would
feel to be a star again, and if I'd ever know.

▪ 10 ▪

Game seven was going to be tough. We all knew that.
We had to head across Lake Washington to take on
Bellevue High. Road games are always hard to win, especially against good teams. They'd come in second in the
state the year before, and most of their guys were back,
ready to make a run for the title. They were undefeated
and were ranked number three by the *Seattle Times*.
There'd be newspaper reporters at the game, and scouts
for major league teams.

The bus ride across the bridge was strangely quiet. A

couple of guys mentioned the 15–4 pasting Bellevue had laid on us the year before, but nobody said anything about getting even. It seemed they were getting ready to have it happen again.

Josh and I sat way in the back. "You know what I like about being a pitcher?" he said as we bounced along in that old school bus.

I laughed. "Blowing a fastball by some guy for strike three."

But he was being serious. "No, not that. I mean that's okay and all. But what I really like is putting the ball right there on the corner of home plate, right between being a strike and a ball. Painting the black, so that nobody knows what it really is, not the umpire and not the hitter. Then I have everybody eating out of my hand. Everybody."

He looked around the bus, and lowered his voice. "These guys don't think we can win. Wheatley doesn't think we can win. But it doesn't matter. Because when my pitches are on the black, the only guy I need is me."

"And a catcher," I said, ribbing him a little. "Unless you plan on catching your own pitches, too."

He didn't laugh. "You're right, Ryan. You're right. I need a catcher." He put his arm around my shoulder and gave me a little shake. "And I've got you, don't I?"

Bellevue is a richer city than Seattle, and their ballpark shows it. There's nothing wrong with Woodland Park, but Bellevue Field is in another world. The grass is a deep green, and it's cross-cut like a major league park. There are real dugouts, real cinder warning tracks, real signs marking the real distances on the fence. Even the bleachers are better. They're solid concrete, they're covered, and they rise steeply behind home plate so that you feel like the people watching are looking down on you.

The ballpark was so impressive it psyched me out a little. I felt that I didn't really belong, that it was too good for me. Other guys felt the same way. We didn't get looser as we warmed up, we got tighter. Everyone except Josh. It was as if the better the park was, the more at home he felt.

Right from the start he was calm. Not relaxed — he was *intensely* calm. Josh's eyes were honed on Selin's mitt like a laser beam on a target.

And that's what his pitches looked like too. Laser beams, heat-seeking missiles. He struck out the side in the first. He struck out the side in the second. The seven hitter led off the third with a bunt single, and a sacrifice bunt from the number eight hitter ended his string of strikeouts. But after the out was recorded at first, Josh took his cap off, smoothed his long dark hair, and struck out the next two batters on six pitches.

Seeing him blow away the Bellevue hitters changed our team. As the Bellevue players walked back to their bench shaking their heads, we started holding our heads a little higher.

In our half of the fifth, we caught a break. Their pitcher retired Van Tassel to open the inning, but then he walked Curtis and Combs. On a 2–0 pitch, Bayne hit a perfect double-play grounder. But the Bellevue shortstop bobbled it and then threw wildly to first. One run scored, and Selin drove in two more with a ringing double to left center.

I went in to catch the bottom of the sixth. From his warm-up pitches, I could see Josh was tiring. He'd been dripping sweat since the first inning, but now he looked cold somehow. All those strikeouts had taken their toll. He'd kept us in the game, given us a chance to win. But could he finish them off?

The inning started okay. The first batter popped up to short. But the number two hitter lined a single to center — a hard hit ball. Then we got lucky. They sent up a pinch hitter, a big muscular guy, and he smacked a rocket down the line at third. Curtis somehow knocked it down, picked it up, and fired it to first for the put-out. It was a great play, because if it had gotten by him it would have been extra bases. Still, the baserunner had moved up to second on the out, and he scored Bellevue's first run when the next batter drilled a hanging curve off the wall in right field for a double. I looked down toward the bullpen and saw Smith throwing. Just seeing him up made my stomach go into knots. He was a good enough pitcher, but he was a freshman, and this game was too much for him. If he came in, we'd lose.

Josh's tempo slowed down incredibly. After every pitch, he'd take a little walk around the mound, shake his arm out. His rhythm was shot, and so was his control. He walked the tying run aboard on four pitches, and then went two balls and no strikes on the next hitter. The Bellevue fans were stomping their feet, and the Bellevue players were up in the dugout. They could sense the kill.

I called time and trotted out to him. His face looked pained, and he kept kicking the dirt. "Forget about everything," I said. "It's just you and me over at the Community Center, and you're throwing me that nasty slider. Okay?"

He looked at me and sort of laughed. "That easy, eh?"

I smiled back. "That easy."

Ten seconds later I was crouching behind the plate, sticking down three fingers. Josh delivered. The awkwardness, the jerkiness in his motion were gone, the liquid grace was back. That slider dipped just as the guy swung. "Strike one!" the umpire bellowed. I popped up and fired the ball back to Josh. He caught it without moving, and it was as if we were back at the Community Center. The batter didn't exist, the baserunners didn't exist. Strike two was a fastball that froze him. The guy went down on a wicked slider that the bottom dropped out of. End of inning, and we still had a two-run lead.

Wheatley came over during our half of the seventh. "You got anything left?" he asked Josh.

"I'm fine," Josh insisted.

Wheatley nodded. "Smith's ready. You can come out if you want."

"I want to finish."

He made a fist in front of his face. "That's the spirit."

I spent the rest of that half-inning laying out a plan. When a pitcher loses it, he usually loses it pretty fast. So I had to figure for the worst. There was a decent chance he'd have no velocity on his fastball, no bite left in his curve or his slider. But if he could spot the ball, if he could get ahead in the count and then get the hitters to swing at bad balls, they'd get themselves out.

We didn't score in our half of the seventh. I pulled the mask over my face, went back behind the plate, and caught Josh's warm-up tosses. "Let's go!" the ump cried. I fired the ball down to second, it went around the horn, and the batter stepped in.

Bellevue's two-three-four hitters were due up. I started the first guy off with a fastball, figuring he'd be taking, and Josh laid one right down the middle. "Strike one!" the ump called. Josh looked in for the sign. I called for another fastball, and I pointed away emphatically. He nodded, and then came with a tempting fastball belt high but about six inches outside. The guy couldn't resist. He swung viciously, but caught the ball way out on the end of his bat and dribbled an easy grounder to Combs at first. One down, two to go.

The next guy was their best hitter, and the most disciplined. I started him out with two fastballs outside. He didn't bite. Behind in the count, there was nothing to do but come in with a pitch. He was all over it, whistling a line drive to center for a solid single.

Their cleanup batter stepped in, representing the tying run. Sweat was streaming from Josh's face. I called for another fastball, figuring he'd be taking on the first pitch. Josh came in with it, belt high, right down the middle. The guy roped a line drive to left center. It bounded between our fielders and went all the way to the wall. The runner from first scored easily, cutting our lead to one, and the hitter could have made third. I don't know why he held up. It was a big break for us — they'd need a hit to score him.

Wheatley walked slowly out of the dugout. "Can you finish?" he asked Josh. Josh nodded. Wheatley turned to me. "What do you think?"

"We can do it," I said.

He looked down at Smith, then looked at Josh. "Okay. Go get 'em."

There were about seventy-five Bellevue fans in the bleachers, and they were stomping and making the noise of a couple hundred. I think that actually worked to our advantage. The batter was anxious, too anxious. We started him off with a fastball outside and high. It's a sucker's pitch and he went for it, fouling it down the right field line. I decided to climb the ladder with him. I called for another fastball, and pointed up. This one Josh put about shoulder high, and the guy swung again, missing it entirely for strike two. He pounded the bat down in disgust.

Keep climbing it, I thought, as I called for another fastball up. Josh came back with a not-so-fast fastball that was about eye level — exactly what I'd wanted. The guy couldn't lay off. Again he caught nothing but air. We'd struck him out without even throwing a strike. Two down.

I popped up and went out to talk to Josh. Van Tassel came in from second to listen. "One more hitter," I told Josh. "Have you got three more pitches left in you?"

He blew out some air. "I don't know, Ryan. I hope so."

"Maybe we don't have to get him out," Van Tassel whispered.

170

"What do you mean?" I asked.

"Let's try to pick the guy off second. He's flat-footed out there, watching, especially after the pitch. I think we can get him."

"All right," I said. "Let's try it." I looked back to Josh. "Throw me a fastball outside."

Josh went into his stretch, delivered. It wasn't quite a pitch-out, but it was a good two feet outside. I was coming out of my crouch as I caught it, and in one motion I fired down to Van Tassel, who'd broken in behind the runner. It was the best throw of my life, a bullet to the shortstop side of the bag. The guy was so stunned he never even slid. Van Tassel slapped the tag on his knee when he was still a yard from the bag. "Out!" the umpire hollered. For a second everyone stood still, too shocked to believe the game was really over, that we'd really won.

That bus ride back was different from the one going. The entire way, guys were shouting and screaming. They were pounding Josh on the back, pounding me on the back, pounding Van Tassel on the back. Then, just as we got off the freeway, Coach Cliff motioned for me to come sit next to him.

"You did a great job," he said.

"Thanks," I replied.

"Listen. I talked to Coach Wheatley, and we both agree that the next time Josh pitches, you're going to catch. First inning to last. How's that sound?"

My face broke into a huge smile. "Sounds great to me!"

"All you've got to do is hit a little, Ryan, and you'll catch him all year. You've earned your chance, kid. Make the most of it."

Part Four

▪ 1 ▪

You made it, Ryan. Now don't let up! Play the string out to the very end. The very end." That's what Josh said every time I saw him. I'd nod as if he was telling me something I didn't already know, but there was no way I was letting up. In the morning when I awoke, I felt strong inside, like every single cell in me was bursting with life. It was a feeling I wanted to keep forever.

I wasn't the only guy on a high. The whole baseball team was. We were the darlings of the school, of the Crown Hill community. We were in first place in the league. We were in the top ten in the state. Those days, even breathing was exciting.

When Josh was on the mound, our wins were almost automatic. All we needed to do was scratch out a run or two and he'd take care of the rest. And we were scoring more than a run or two. Van Tassel and Curtis were reaching base. Combs, Bayne, and Hernandes were pounding out extra base hits the way drummers in a marching band pound out a beat.

I was tight at the plate the first couple of games I started. I wasn't quite sure what Coach Cliff meant when he said I had to *hit a little*. But hitting is contagious. You see the guys at the top of the lineup sending line drives all over the park, and you start to believe you can do it too. I banged out at least one hit in every game Josh pitched, and two hits — including a double — against Ingraham, not bad for somebody hitting in the eighth spot in the lineup.

The most amazing thing was the way Chris Selin acted toward me. He had every reason to be burned. I was taking half his innings, half his at-bats. I was catching the star pitcher. I wouldn't have blamed him if he didn't even look at me. But if I stroked a hit or scored a run, or even if I made an out, Selin was always there, cheering me on if I'd done well, picking me up if I was down. It wasn't easy for him. I could see it in his eyes. Still, he did it.

The runs we scored for Josh made calling his games a snap. Fastball in, fastball out. Mix in an occasional change or curveball in the early innings, then call for that wicked slider to blow them away late.

Not that I'm trying to take credit for his success. A catcher can call a perfect game, but if the pitcher doesn't pitch, it means nothing. Josh pitched. Josh was awesome. It was as if he were a big jungle cat and the batters were little mice he was toying with. He won his next four starts 6–2, 8–0, 9–1, and 5–1. I caught every inning.

When you're a catcher, you're into each pitch of the game, no matter what the score. That's not true of anybody else. With a big lead the infielders don't crouch

176

quite so low and the outfielders start singing songs to themselves. Whenever I saw a guy drifting off, I'd motion for him to move a step to the right or a step to the left, back a little or in a little, not because he needed to move, but to wake him up. It's like being a puppet master, in a way. You point your finger and your left fielder moves. It's a good feeling, controlling things. A real good feeling.

But Josh started only half the games. David Reule started the other half, and when Reule was on the mound, Wheatley had Chris Selin behind the plate and me back on the bench.

It's hard to say how I felt about that. I wanted to play. Even if I was banged up or sore from catching Josh, I wanted to be out there. You learn from watching guys, though. And I'd learned from Selin. So no matter how his game went — whether he hit a home run or struck out, whether he cut down a base-stealer or had a passed ball — I was in his corner. I'd like to think I backed him the same way he backed me. I know I tried.

Reule's games were murder to watch. My stomach would churn from the first pitch to the last. His fastball was just okay. His curveball broke, but not sharply, and it had no zip at all. It seemed like every inning the other team would have a couple of guys on base.

But Reule was a competitor. Roosevelt beat him 7–4, dropping us into a tie with O'Dea. In his other starts, though, he got the outs when he needed them. Or if he didn't, then Wilkerson or Smith came in and got them for him. I don't think we won any of those games by more than two runs, and twice we had to come back in the last inning to win, but we won.

We needed those wins, every one of them, because O'Dea kept on winning too. It was like one of those stare-downs you have with your friends when you're a kid. Only one of us could go on to the state tournament. Who was going to blink first?

When the showdown game was three weeks off, I was sure the league championship would be settled — one way or the other — before we met. It didn't seem possible for both of us to win out. Either they'd drop a few or we would. But they took care of their business and we took care of ours. When I looked at the schedule after Josh shut out Nathan Hale 3–0 on a two-hitter, there was only one game left to play: O'Dea, at their field, with the regional championship — and a spot in the state tournament — on the line.

▪ 2 ▪

I didn't like our chances. Not with Reule on the mound. For a while I second-guessed Wheatley, thinking he should have thrown Reule against Nathan Hale, and saved Josh for O'Dea. But that would have been risky, too. There was no guarantee Reule would have beaten Nathan Hale, and we didn't need to face O'Dea coming off a loss. Besides, if you've got a rhythm going that's working, you keep it.

Having to sit out the championship game played at Josh's mind. Friday during lunch he kept talking about how in California things were different. "With our record, we'd be in the state tournament even if we came in second," he complained. "And it's a double elimination tournament besides."

"Washington is smaller," I said.

He glowered. "Yeah, well, it's not fair."

Saturday was one of those May days that tease you. When the sun was out, it was almost like summer. But when the clouds covered the sun, you'd swear it was January.

O'Dea played on an old field on Capitol Hill. Sections of the outfield fence were missing. The infield grass was spotty; there were holes in the screen behind the plate. The bleachers held about fifty people, so the fans — and there were a couple of hundred — sat along the foul lines to watch. None of that mattered. The feel of a championship game was in the air.

During their batting practice Number Forty put on a show. The drives he hit seemed to have after-burners — line shots into the left and right center alleys. He set the tone for all O'Dea's hitters. They were loose and confident.

"They act like champions," Josh whispered to me. "I'd give anything to pitch today. Anything."

Reule, who'd been shaky in his last outings, came out throwing strong. He kept the ball low, and the O'Dea guys were overeager, pounding grounder after grounder into the dirt. They scratched out a couple of singles in the first two innings, but that was all. We didn't do any better, though. The O'Dea right-hander mowed us down like we were toy soldiers.

The third can be a dangerous inning for a pitcher. The top of the order is coming back up again, and the second time around good hitters have a better idea of what to expect. The O'Dea leadoff guy smacked a hard grounder right at Ruben. The ball kicked off the heel of Ruben's glove, caught him hard in the chest, then trickled toward second base. Runner on first. The number two guy tried to sacrifice the runner along, but Reule came inside with a fastball that nicked him in the arm. "Take your base!" the umpired yelled, and O'Dea was really in business.

Number Forty stepped to the plate, dug himself a little hole with his back foot, settled in, and nodded that he was ready. Reule checked the runners, then delivered a curve that dipped outside for a ball. His second pitch was another curve, this time just low. "Don't give in to him," Josh whispered. "Don't give in."

But he did. Reule's 2–0 pitch had nothing on it, a fastball right down the pike. Number Forty uncoiled. The ball soared skyward, a tremendous drive to straightaway center.

Bayne turned one way, then another. He got his feet tangled and fell. But it didn't matter. The ball cleared the fence in dead center by a good thirty feet. Forty rumbled around the bases as the O'Dea crowd cheered wildly. We were down 3–0.

The guys didn't give up, though. They fought back, scratching out a single run in the fourth on a double, a stolen base, and a sac fly. Then in the fifth O'Dea gave us a run on a walk and a three-base error, a routine fly ball their right fielder butchered.

Reule held O'Dea in check through five. But you could see he was tiring. In between innings Josh cornered Wheatley. "I could pitch an inning or two," he said. "I know I could."

Wheatley shook his head. "Forget it. I won't do anything that might hurt your arm."

Josh slumped down on the seat next to me, stuffed sunflower seeds in his mouth, and machine-gunned the shells out.

In our half of the sixth, Wheatley sent me out to warm up Wilkerson. It was a good move, because when O'Dea came to the plate Reule walked the leadoff batter on four pitches. He got the next guy to pop up, but the hitter after that drilled a single through the box. Wheatley walked slowly to the mound, then called for Wilkerson. I went back to my seat on the bench next to Josh.

It was Number Forty again at the plate. "Is this guy always up?" Josh muttered as we watched Wilkerson take his final warm-up tosses from the mound. "Get him out, Randy! Get him out!"

Forty dug himself a toe hole. Wilkerson stretched. Suddenly I couldn't look. I put my head down and stared at the sunflower seed shells on the ground.

I couldn't close my ears though, and at the crack of the bat my head jerked up. Forty had sent a ringing double into the left center alley. This time Bayne played it well, and only one run scored. Wilkerson got the next two guys, but we were behind 4–2, and we were down to our last at-bat. Three more outs and our season was over.

As the guys came in, Wheatley clapped his hands together. "Let's get going!" he shouted. "A little spirit here!"

A couple of guys — Ruben, Nelson — let out a cheer. But it was fake. You play a whole season; you win a slew of games; but the last one — the one that knocks you out of the tournament — is the one you remember.

Before he headed to the third base coach's box, Wheatley came over to me. "If we get deep enough into the inning, you're going to pinch-hit."

Josh heard. "Check the card," he said. "And get your bat."

My heart was pounding like crazy as I walked over to where the lineup card was posted. Nelson was scheduled to bat fifth, and he was slumping. He'd struck out three times in the game, and he was zero for his last sixteen.

"Nelson's batting fifth," I said softly to Josh when I returned.

"It'll be for him," he said, then he paused. "If you get up, Ryan, the game will be on the line. Start thinking about it now. You've got to be ready."

You find out about yourself in moments like that. And what I found out surprised me. I knew I'd changed since I'd met Josh. But right then I found out just how much. Because I wanted to get up. I wanted the chance to bat with the game, with the season, on the line. There was no way I would have wanted to be in a spot like that before Josh. No way at all.

It wasn't that I was confident I'd get the big hit. Sitting on the bench, my hands working the handle of my bat, I knew the chances were good that I'd make an out. But that was okay. I could live with it. I wanted the chance.

Bayne started the inning by working a walk, but then Selin popped to left for the first out, and Jamaal Wilsey struck out on three pitches.

Carlos Hernandes straggled up to the plate, looking for all the world like the last out. O'Dea's pitcher delivered a fastball right down the heart for a strike. Carlos stepped out, tugged on his gloves, stepped back in. The second pitch was a fastball in on the fists. Hernandes swung weakly, blooping a little flare, a dying quail that dropped in front of the right fielder for a single. The tying runs were aboard.

I looked over at Wheatley as Nelson walked toward the batter's box. For an instant I thought I'd figured wrong, that Nelson would bat. But then Wheatley came out of the third base box, pointing at me and waving Nelson back to the bench.

"Be hacking," Josh whispered as I grabbed my helmet.

I passed Nelson as he headed back to the bench. I could see in his eyes that he was glad to be off the hook.

I took a few practice swings and then stepped in. Josh's words went through my mind over and over. *All right*, I thought, *let's make it happen — now.*

The right-hander stretched, checked the runners, fired. I'd like to say I saw the ball clearly, that it came in as big as a watermelon, but that'd be a lie. The truth is it was just a blur. I swung anyway, and I'm glad I did, because I caught that ball on the sweet spot and it took off, a rocket down the line in left. The only question was whether it would stay fair. As I raced toward first I watched the ball hooking, hooking, hooking.

And then, the magic words. "Fair ball!" the umpire shouted, and he twirled his finger in the air to signal a home run. The guys on the bench exploded, Wheatley exploded, our fans exploded. When I crossed home plate my teammates crowded around me, banging me on the top of the helmet and sweeping me toward the dugout.

It felt great, but the whole time I was looking for Josh. I couldn't figure where he was, why he wasn't sharing the moment with me. Then I saw him down in the bullpen warming up. "Get your gear on," Wheatley said to me as Bethel Santos popped up to end our half of the inning. "You're catching the bottom of the seventh."

If I'd been managing the team, I'd have brought Josh in right away. Why warm him up if you're not going to use him? But Wheatley sent Wilkerson back out there.

There never was a chance. Wilkerson is a decent pitcher, but there's no way he could close out O'Dea. Not in their ballpark. Not for the championship. There was just no way.

His first two pitches were about three feet high. The third one was in the dirt. Ball four sailed clear to the backstop. Wheatley came out, took the ball from him, and motioned for Josh, who quickly trotted to the mound. "Let's do it," Wheatley said as he handed Josh the ball.

"It's done," Josh answered.

I've never seen eyes look the way his eyes looked that inning. They were so focused, it was scary. I knew what to call for, too. Those eyes told me, without a word being exchanged. Fastballs. Nothing but fastballs. Pure heat. Pitcher against batter. Here it is. Hit it if you can.

They couldn't. Nine pitches. Nine strikes, the last three blown right by Number Forty, who swung so hard at the final pitch he fell down. And then we were all at the mound, jumping on Josh till we knocked him down. We had done it. We had beaten O'Dea! We were going to state. It was like a dream, a wild and crazy dream with the wildest and craziest ending. I'll live my whole life and never be part of anything more exciting.

A huge headline blazed across the prep pages of the Sunday *Seattle Times*: **Something Special on Crown Hill**. It was all about Josh and how close he'd come to beating O'Dea in football. *Now he's done it on the diamond*, the last sentence read, *and don't be surprised if his fabulous right arm leads the Vikings all the way to the Promised Land.*

Monday at school Josh's face was lit up like a Christmas tree. As guys on the team passed him on their way to class, they'd make little salaaming motions like he was their lord and master. Kolas Chang grabbed his right arm and started kissing it.

"Knock it off!" Josh said, smiling.

▪ 3 ▪

Sometimes I think what happened had to happen, like a crash of two trains speeding in opposite directions on the same track. But at other times it seems as if there were places where either one of them — Josh or Monica — could have turned off. Take that day. Monica could have let Josh ride high. She could have let him have his moment.

She could have, but she didn't.

Ms. Hurley had a challenge going in our English class. If anyone found something badly written in a newspaper or magazine, they could read it to the class and get extra points. Monica had her hand up first thing that day.

"Listen to this," she said, her arm over the back of her chair, her eyes darting around the room. "It's from yesterday's paper — the sports section." Then she read: *"Don't be surprised if his fabulous right arm leads the Vikings all the way to the Promised Land."*

Ms. Hurley's face broke into a smile.

"What's so funny?" Josh demanded, his face reddening.

Monica grinned. "It's ridiculous!"

"There is nothing ridiculous about it," Josh insisted. "We can take the state."

Monica shook her head. "I'm not talking about baseball. I'm talking about the writing."

"It's a mixed metaphor," Ms. Hurley explained, in her best teacher's voice. "It was the Jews who were trying to get to the Promised Land, not the Vikings."

186

Still Josh glared, red-faced.

"Look, Josh," Ms. Hurley went on. "Imagine Leif Ericson wearing his little horned helmet. Now imagine him wandering around the desert with Moses, and you'll see why the sentence is silly."

A lot of kids smiled then, but Josh stayed stonily silent, his arms folded across his chest.

Monica noticed. She turned toward Josh. "You *have* heard of Moses, haven't you? You know, the guy in the Bible. God gives him the Ten Commandments. Maybe you saw the movie."

I'd never heard her more sarcastic.

"Are you calling me stupid?" Josh snapped.

The smile disappeared from Monica's face. "If the shoe fits . . . ," she said, her voice trailing off.

"That's enough, Monica!" Ms. Hurley interjected, her voice louder than I'd heard it all year. "More than enough."

Monica held her hands up in front of her. "Sorry," she said. But there was still the hint of a smirk on her face.

At practice that day everyone was chattering, full of good spirits. Everyone except Josh. He seemed a million miles away. I knew what was on his mind.

"Don't let Monica get to you," I said as we walked home after practice. "That's just her way."

"Yeah, well, we all have our ways, don't we?" he muttered.

▪ 4 ▪

The next day Coach Wheatley called us together. "You're good baseball players," he said. "Every one of you. But the other fifteen teams have good baseball players too. Talent won't be enough. The team that wins will be the team that keeps its focus, the team that does the little things right." He took a deep breath. "You don't get many chances in life to be a champion, gentlemen. The golden ring is dangling right in front of our eyes. Let's grab it."

That practice was crisp. The infielders had their gloves in the dirt and their throws were on the money. The outfielders chased down flies into the gap. In the batting cage, guys were swinging at good pitches and hitting the ball where it was pitched. It felt so good, so exactly right, that I didn't want practice to end.

I took a long shower that afternoon. I stuck my head right under the nozzle and let the water pound onto the top of my head. I must have stood there for a long time, because when I opened my eyes the shower room was empty. I turned the nozzle off and headed to my locker. The only guy still around was Jamaal Wilsey, and he was zipping up his bag. As I dried myself off, he asked me if I thought we could win the whole thing.

"You bet we can," I said. "And we will."

He nodded. "I think so too." Then he looked me right in the eye. "And you know what else I think? I think it's going to come down to you."

That took me aback, because it was a feeling I'd had more than once. "How do you figure?" I asked.

"You're our number one pinch-hitter now," he said. "No doubt about it. The way you went up there and smacked that home run, it was like you had ice water in your veins."

"I don't know about that," I answered. "I was plenty nervous."

He laughed. "There are ten guys on this team who wouldn't have been able to swing the bat in that situation. I know because I'm one of them. You came up big in a big spot, Ryan. If a game is on the line again, Coach will want you at the plate."

"You really think so?" I said.

He pushed the door open, then turned and looked back at me. "I don't think it. I *know* it."

The door swung closed behind him and I was alone. I had to smile at how unbelievable it all seemed. Me, the guy who had been afraid to try out, and now my teammates were hoping that *I'd* be the one to step up to the plate with the state title on the line. Even more amazing, I was hoping for it too. The pressure was like a drug in my veins. I wanted more.

I closed my eyes, and suddenly I wasn't in the locker room anymore. I was at Cheney Stadium, playing on an emerald green cross-cut ball field. I was gunning down baserunners trying to steal, blasting RBI doubles into the power alleys, catching the third strike for the third out in the bottom of the seventh.

Then the door burst open and the night janitor was

standing there. I just about jumped out of my skin. "What are you doing in here, kid?" he asked, and I could tell I'd scared him, too. "Get your pants on and go home."

"Right," I said, pulling my jeans up. "Sorry."

When I stepped outside, a gray mist had settled in. The school felt strange, too quiet and too empty.

That's why seeing the two guys startled me. They were maybe a hundred yards ahead of me, and they were moving in fits and starts down the hallway, hugging the wall as they went. Every so often they'd look around to see if anyone was watching them.

When they looked my way, I stepped into a classroom doorway so they couldn't see me. I was a little scared, but it wasn't just fear. They didn't want to be seen, and that made me want to spy on them. The next few minutes were like one of those old detective movies. They'd move forward, and I'd move forward. They'd stop and I'd stop.

Finally they reached the end of the last hallway and started up the path leading past the music portable. That ended my detective work. I usually went home that way, but there were all kinds of bushes and trees up there. Whatever those guys were up to, it was no good, and I didn't want any part of it or them. So I turned right and headed out onto Sixty-fifth. That route was longer, but just seeing cars and other people made me feel better.

I got across the street before I thought of Monica. Then I stopped dead in my tracks, my whole body tense. She was up there, at the top of the path, alone in the music portable.

That's when it hit me. The straight shoulders, the little

190

bounce on the balls of the feet. I hadn't seen the face, but I knew that walk.

I gave myself a little shake and told myself that even if they were planning something, Monica was gone. It was later than usual, and I hadn't heard any music. She was home. She was safe.

I started toward my own home, but I hadn't gone more than ten steps before I turned around. I had to know for sure.

By then it was deep twilight. I bounded up the stairs and re-entered the main campus. I half-walked and half-ran down the hallways. The air was so thick that my own footsteps sounded far away and muffled, like a blanket was over everything. As I came up to the portable, I heard something. I didn't know what. But something. I crouched and peered through the window, the same way I had that first day when I'd discovered Monica playing.

At first I couldn't see anything, but slowly my eyes adjusted to the darkness. When I finally could see, I couldn't make sense of what I was seeing. Two guys wearing Halloween wolf masks were kneeling on the ground, their hands grabbing and tearing at something on the floor. I cupped my hands against the side of my head and looked harder. That's when I saw that that *something* on the floor was Monica.

Her blouse had been torn open. One of the guys had her around the neck while the other guy had his hands on her pants and was yanking and pulling. She was fighting back, kicking and squirming and biting. I could hear choked screams.

I leaned back away from the window. My heart was racing. I couldn't move; I couldn't breathe. I felt like running, running down the hill and back to my house. No one would ever know I'd been there.

I think I even decided that that was what I'd do. That I'd run straight home, climb the stairs to my room, close the door, and turn on my radio. That's what I would have done the year before, and I could feel that other person inside me, pulling me away. But I wasn't that person anymore, and I didn't run.

I took a deep breath and then threw open the door. "Leave her alone!" I shouted.

For one second everything stopped. The two of them looked at me, then let go of her. A second later the closest one was charging at me. I held my hands up in front of my face expecting fists to rain down on me, but all he wanted was to get past me. He grabbed me, and I recognized the grip of the hand, and he pulled me forward, spun me around, and shoved me toward the center of the room. I hit a desk hard and fell. When I looked up the second guy was running out the door behind him.

Monica was maybe ten feet away, weeping softly. I crawled toward her. "You okay?" I whispered, embarrassed by her half-naked body, glad that it was as dark as it was, not knowing what to do or say.

She didn't answer. Instead she pulled her knees up to her chest and started rocking back and forth. I took off my coat and put it over her. I laid my hand on her shoulder, but she shook convulsively at the touch. I took my hand away.

I don't know how long she rocked back and forth. Maybe five minutes, probably less. I do know that the room was almost completely dark when she finally spoke. "Look away," she whispered hoarsely. I turned my head and I could hear her pull her clothes back on as best she could.

"Do you have a handkerchief?"

I pulled one out of my back pocket and handed it to her. She wiped her face.

"What can I do?" I asked.

"Walk me to Sixty-fifth," she said softly. "I'll be okay once I get there."

I would have gladly done more. I would have let her cry on my shoulder. I would have walked her all the way home. I would have bought her something to drink, something to eat.

But that's all she asked for, so that's all I did.

When I opened my own front door the house smelled like tomatoes and garlic. "Is that you, Ryan?" my mom called from the kitchen. "You're late."

"Sorry," I said, "we had a team meeting after practice."

"I hope you're hungry. I made spaghetti for dinner."

I went into the kitchen and gave her a kiss. Then my eyes fell on a saucepan filled with thick tomato sauce and bits of sausage and mushroom. A wave of nausea came over me.

I stepped back. "Actually," I said, "I don't think I can eat anything. I don't feel good."

She put the lid down on the sauce pan. "Ryan, I've been waiting dinner especially for you."

"I'm sorry, Mother," I said. "But my stomach aches and my head hurts."

My father came downstairs. "Did I hear you come in, Ryan?"

"He doesn't feel good," my mother said, and she put her hand up toward my forehead to check for a fever.

I pulled away. "I'm just tired. All I want to do is go to my room, maybe read a little, then sleep."

"Anything go wrong at practice?" my father asked.

"No," I said. "Nothing went wrong. I'm just tired."

He nodded. "Well, we'll see you in the morning, then."

I hadn't lied to them. I was tired, more tired than I've ever been in my life, but as soon as I closed the door to my room, I knew I couldn't sleep. I turned my reading light on, then went to my window to look out.

I don't know how long I stared at Josh's window, trying to make sense of what he had done. I tried to get my mind around it in a dozen different ways, but there was no doing it, no doing it.

I returned to my bed, flicked off the light, and lay there in the dark, staring at the ceiling. *What was going to happen next?* That was the question that kept going through my mind. *What was going to happen next?*

▪ 5 ▪

Josh and I never walked to school together. He was late a lot, and even when he wasn't, he was barely on time, and I liked to get going early. But that next morning I sat on the step at the bottom of his porch, waiting for him to come out of his house.

He smiled when he saw me, a big toothy smile. "Hey, Ryan!" he called out in a too-loud, too-happy voice, "What's happening?"

"Nothing much, Josh," I answered. "What's happening with you?"

"Nothing at all," he said, trying so hard to sound natural that he seemed incredibly unnatural.

We walked along for a block. He was going on and on about the baseball team and the state tournament.

"Listen," I interrupted, "what do you say we skip first period and get something at Larsen's?"

He grinned at me. "I didn't think you ever cut class. I thought you were Mr. Straight A's."

I was tired of playing games. "I've never gotten straight A's in my life, Josh. And we need to talk right away."

The smile disappeared. "All right."

When we reached Larsen's we got some doughnuts and mocha and found a table in the corner.

"I love their stuff," Josh said, biting into his doughnut, his voice cheerful again.

"Look," I said, "I know it was you."

He sipped his mocha. "You know what was me?"

195

I grimaced. "Cut it out, will you? Don't play games with me."

But he persisted. "You're the one who's playing games. I don't have a clue what you're talking about."

"I'm talking about the Halloween masks your father never threw away. I'm talking about what you and who-ever was with you did to Monica Roby yesterday."

That got him. He leaned toward me, the smile gone. "Keep your voice down, will you!"

After that we both spoke in whispers.

"What were you going to do to her, anyway?" I asked.

He scowled. "We weren't going to rape her, if that's what you're asking. All we were going to do was pants her, scare her a little. Then you came busting in and ruined everything."

"How could you be so stupid?" I said, frustrated.

"It was a prank, a joke, that's all. A way to get back at her for the stuff she's done to me. It should have been over in about a minute, and it would have been if she hadn't fought."

"What did you think she was going to do, Josh? Let you strip her naked and do nothing?"

"I didn't think she'd fight like that," he snapped. He held his hand out. "She bit me so hard my hand still hurts."

I looked out the window and saw a long line of cars waiting for the light to change on Eightieth.

"Listen," I said at last. "It's not going to take her long to figure out it was you. And when she does, she'll go straight to Haskin. She might be there right now."

"Did she say my name yesterday?"

I shook my head. "No."

His jaw tightened. "So how come you're so sure she knows it's me?"

"Because it's obvious." I paused. "You should go to Haskin this morning and explain that it was supposed to be a joke, but that it somehow got way out of hand, and that you're sorry. He might go easy on you."

Josh laughed mockingly. "He won't go easy on me. He'll suspend me, and Wheatley will kick me off the team. That can't happen, Ryan, not now. Not with the tournament coming up. Those major league scouts have got to see me pitch. They've got to. My future is on the line."

"I'm telling you: She knows it's you."

He leaned back. "You don't know for sure she's going to report this. And even if she does, even if she says it was me, what does it matter? Lots of guys don't like her. She can't prove anything. Nobody can prove anything." He paused. "Unless you talk."

His words hung there like a kite stuck in a tree.

I took a deep breath. "I'm not going to say anything. But I still think —"

"Don't think," he snapped. He finished off his mocha, then stood. "You're making a big deal out of nothing. I scared her a little. Paid her back a little. That's all. It's over."

We walked straight to school then. Neither of us spoke, and when we reached the main hallway we went our separate ways without so much as a nod.

I wanted Josh to be right. I wanted to believe nothing had happened. During the passing periods that morning I searched for Monica. I wanted to see her walking down the center of the hallway the way she always did, a smile on her face, a troupe of followers behind her. I looked and looked, but I couldn't find her.

By the time fourth period rolled around I was certain she wasn't at school. As I headed toward Ms. Hurley's room, I spotted Josh. He was laughing loudly, his arm around Rita Hall. I had a sudden feeling of revulsion for him. I couldn't bear the thought of seeing him grin his way through English, playing the part of the total innocent.

I'd already missed half of one class that day, so I decided to go ahead and skip another one entirely. I headed across Fifteenth and over to Salmon Bay Park.

I sat on one of the picnic benches that looks down on the playground. A few young mothers were there, pushing their toddlers on the swings, helping them climb the monkey bars. They glanced up at me suspiciously, wondering what I was doing.

As I watched the little kids play, I thought about the words Josh had used to describe what he had done. *A prank. A joke.* They were the wrong words. They described harmless things, childish things — things that are quickly done and quickly forgotten. But Monica wouldn't forget what Josh had done to her, not ever. And I wouldn't forget either, not for as long as I lived. Then I realized what he was really telling me: that he *could* forget about it, and that he would.

I thought back over the year, over things Josh had said and done. What had happened in the music portable — it fit. It was like the final piece of a jigsaw puzzle. The picture had been there all along. But I'd been so close to it, I hadn't been able to see it. Or maybe I hadn't wanted to see it.

I suddenly felt cold. I looked up at the sky and saw that clouds had covered the sun. Pretty soon the poplars were tossing back and forth, and the mothers on the playground were herding their children home.

I would have loved a downpour — thunder and lightning and torrential rain. I would have let it drench me to the bone, the way Monica had during that storm in fifth grade. But it was May, not February, and instead of a winter storm it was the briefest of spring showers, over almost before it had started.

I walked back to school. I sat through Mrs. Beck's class and had just begun to read in Mr. Woodruff's when the classroom phone rang.

Mr. Woodruff picked it up. "Yes, he's here . . . Okay. I'll send him right down." He hung up, turned toward me. "Ryan, Mr. Haskin wants to see you in his office."

Kids around me *oohhed* and *aahhed* mockingly.

"Should I bring my books?" I asked.

Mr. Woodruff nodded. "You'd better."

When I reached the office Mrs. Bruch had me sit. "He's got some parents in there now," she said, smiling. "I don't suppose you mind missing a few minutes of class while he finishes up."

"I'll try to survive," I answered, trying to join in her joke.

But a moment later the phone on her desk rang. She put her hand over the receiver. "He wants you to go right in," she said.

I walked to Haskin's door, tapped on it.

"Come in," I heard from within.

Haskin was behind his big oak desk, leaning back in his swivel chair. Facing him were a man and a woman. The man stood as soon as I entered — a short, balding man. He stuck out his hand. "I'm John Roby," he said. My mouth went dry as I shook his hand. "This is my wife, Christine."

She smiled up at me. Looking at her was like looking at Monica in thirty years. The same strong face, only a little wrinkled. The same shining eyes, only somehow sadder.

Haskin motioned for me to take the remaining seat as Mr. Roby sat down again. For an awkward twenty seconds or so, no one spoke. Then Mr. Roby cleared his throat.

"I asked Mr. Haskin to have you come down here so that my wife and I could thank you personally for what you did for our daughter. It was very brave of you."

I wanted to shrink away, to disappear. "All I did was open the door," I said softly.

"I thank God you did open the door," Mrs. Roby put

in, reaching out to take my hand in hers. "I can't even think what might have happened if you hadn't."

I couldn't look at her, so I fixed my eyes on a bit of white on the carpet. No one said anything for a long time.

Finally Mr. Roby stood. "I guess that about does it for today," he said to Mr. Haskin.

Haskin nodded. "I'll get in touch with you as soon as we learn anything."

"Good. I'll be waiting for your call."

Mr. Roby shook my hand again. So did Mrs. Roby. Then he opened the door for his wife and the two of them were gone.

I stood and looked at Haskin, who was sitting in his big chair again. "Should I go back to class now?"

He shook his head. "Sit down, Ryan. I'd like to talk to you for a minute."

He rocked back and forth in his chair, rocked and chewed on the end of his pen and stared at me. I felt more and more uncomfortable as the seconds ticked by. Finally he stopped rocking, leaned forward, tapped his pen on his desk, and then pointed it at me. "Who did it, Ryan?"

I felt my face flush. "I don't know," I stammered. "They were wearing masks."

"I know all about the masks," he answered. "But there are other ways to know people than by seeing their faces. So I'll ask you again. Who did it?"

"I told you. I don't know."

"No idea at all."

201

"None," I said.

He ran his fingertips over his lips. "You did a good thing, Ryan, saving that girl. A very good thing. Don't undo it by lying. The police have been called. A detective will be talking to you. Think about what you're going to say. This wasn't somebody's homework that got copied. This was a criminal assault."

▪ 7 ▪

I waited for the bell ending school, then headed over toward the gym to change for practice. My mind was still back with Haskin, so when I felt the hand on my shoulder, I jumped.

It was Josh. He grabbed me by the elbow and pulled me behind some bushes along the side of the gym.

"What happened?"

I told him about Monica's parents and the police.

"Did my name come up?"

I shook my head.

"Good, good."

"Josh, what am I going to say to the police?"

His eyes widened. "What do you mean, *What are you going to say?* You're not going to say anything."

"It's not that simp —"

Right then David Reule's face peered in at us, stopping

me midsentence. "Hey, what are you guys doing in there?" he called.

"Nothing," Josh answered, and as we stepped out a big smile covered his face.

"I don't know about this," Reule razzed. "Two guys alone in the bushes together . . ."

Josh playfully got Reule in a headlock. "You keep quiet, David. Don't tell anybody our little secret!" The two of them went into the locker room side by side, both of them laughing.

I was terrible at practice. In the batting cage I missed just about everything, and during infield practice I hobbled throws to the plate I normally would have caught no sweat. The only good thing was that Wheatley was in his office poring over the stats on Chehalis, our next opponent.

Around five o'clock Coach Cliff blew his whistle and we headed to the lockers. The shower area is shaped like a T. When I saw Josh at one end, I turned and went down as far as I could away from him.

I got a good shower nozzle, not one that feels like a thousand needles are pricking your body. I soaped up, closed my eyes, and let the water pour over me.

Carlos Hernandes came in about a minute later. As I was rinsing off, he asked if I knew Monica Roby.

"Sure," I said. "Everybody knows her."

He grinned. "Some guys stripped her yesterday up in the music portable. Word is they got her good."

"Where did you hear that?" I asked, trying to sound calm.

"My girlfriend is an office assistant. She heard Haskin talking to Monica's parents." He snorted. "Monica thought they were going to rape her, and maybe they were, though I can't imagine anybody wanting to have sex with her. Anyway, my girlfriend says Monica's so flipped out she's not coming back to school."

"Really," I said.

Hernandes opened his mouth and let water fill it. Then he spit it all out. "I never liked that Monica," he said. "She thinks she's so great. It's about time somebody put her in her place."

Mike Nelson came up then. "Put who in her place?" he asked.

I didn't stick around to hear Hernandes's answer. I had to get away from there, away from the steam and the heat and the talk. I shut off my shower, hustled to my locker, dressed quickly, and walked straight home.

As I headed up the walkway to my house, I sensed something was different. I didn't know what, but something. I opened the front door, and Grandpa Kevin was sitting on the sofa. He stood, a big smile on his face. "Hey, Ryan, good to see you."

I felt a surge of joy. I stuck out my hand, but he pulled me to him and gave me a big hug. "Maybe you're too old for hugs, but I'm not," he said.

"What are you doing here?" I asked, once he let go.

"What am I doing here? You think my grandson is going to play for the state title and I'd miss it? And no sooner do I arrive than a lady detective comes to the door and tells us you're a hero."

He looked to my mother and father, who were both beaming at me. All the excitement drained out of me as my mother began speaking.

"She told us what you did. She's coming back later to talk to you personally." She paused. "Ryan, why didn't you say something yesterday? Weren't you ever going to tell us?"

"There's nothing to tell," I muttered.

"What do you mean, there's nothing to tell?" my father put in. "You were very brave."

The three of them stood there gaping at me as if I was a hero. I wanted to disappear, to go back outside and not come in until it was midnight and they were asleep. I couldn't think of one thing to say, but it seemed we were going to stand there until I came up with something. Grandpa Kevin rescued me.

"I'm hungry, Caroline," he said. "And I bet Ryan is hungry, too. How about if we eat some of that lasagna you've been cooking, before the detective comes back."

That was an awful dinner. I tried to talk baseball with Grandpa Kevin, and he tried to talk it with me. We both tried to be excited about the tournament coming up. But it was no good. Monica Roby might as well have been sitting at the table.

We were finishing our cake when the knock on the door came. "I'll get it," my father said excitedly. I heard him talking at the front door, heard a woman's voice answer him.

"Ryan," he called to me. "Can you come out here now?"

In the front room stood a young blondish woman. She looked more like a teacher than a detective. But when we shook hands, I was surprised by the strength of her grip. "I'm Detective Denise Langford," she said.

"Ryan Ward," I answered.

"Sit down, please," my mother said, coming in from the kitchen. "Would you like coffee or cake or anything?"

"If you've got coffee made, I'll drink it," Detective Langford answered.

There was a little polite chitchat. I kept waiting for my parents to leave, for Grandpa Kevin to leave. I think Detective Langford was waiting for them to go. I don't know when it hit me that they weren't leaving, but when it did, I went cold all over.

"Well," Detective Langford said, taking out a little yellow notebook, "shall we get started?" My mother smiled at me, and my father gave me a nod of encouragement. They were so proud they were just about bursting.

I began by telling her about my home run, and how Wilsey had said what he'd said, and how I'd gone into a little trance. Then I told the rest of it. As I spoke, she scribbled away.

"You were a good citizen," she said when I finished. "The kind of citizen every community needs."

"Thanks," I muttered.

She made a tent with her hands and tapped her fingers together. "Now I'm going to ask you to be an even better citizen. I'm going to ask you to give me the names of the boys who attacked Miss Roby."

I felt my palms go clammy. "I told you. I didn't recognize them."

She flipped through her notebook. "And I heard you. You said you didn't recognize them when you first saw them. You said you didn't recognize them when they ran up toward the portable. You said you didn't recognize them when they were in the portable. You said you didn't recognize them as they ran away." She smiled bitingly. "In fact, you said you didn't recognize them so many times that I'm sure you did. What do you think about that?"

My father rose out of his chair. First there was a look of shock on his face, then anger. "Wait a second here! Wait one second! Are you accusing my son of lying?"

Waves of heat were moving up and down my body.

Detective Langford kept her eyes on me. "Your son is telling the truth, but he's not telling all of it."

My father turned to me. "Do you know anything else, Ryan? Anything you haven't told Detective Langford?"

I shook my head. "They were wearing masks, Dad. How could I recognize them?"

Detective Langford kept her eyes on me. "Maybe you didn't have to recognize them," she said.

"Now what's that supposed to mean?" my father asked.

"It means that maybe Ryan was in on it. Maybe he was the lookout but changed his mind when things got a little too rough." She looked back to me. "Is that what happened, Ryan?"

"That's enough!" my father said, jumping to his feet. "My boy saves a girl from maybe being raped, and you accuse him of being a criminal! I think it's time for you to leave our house."

Detective Langford still kept her eyes on me. "You shape your own world, young man. If you tell the truth, justice will be done. If you don't, it won't be." She stood, handed me a card with her name and telephone number on it, nodded curtly to my parents, and left.

Once she was gone, my father and mother spent about fifteen minutes taking turns saying how outrageous she was to have insinuated I was a liar. "I want you to know," my dad said, and I could see his love for me in his eyes, "I want you to know that your mother and I believe you, one hundred percent. We know you, and we know that you would never hold back the truth in a matter of importance. Never. Do you understand what I'm saying?"

I nodded. My mom hugged me then, and when I started to pull away she pulled me even tighter. Finally she let me go.

It was Grandpa Kevin's turn. "Ryan, can you give me a hand moving my suitcase downstairs?" he said. "I don't know what I was thinking when I put my things in your room. If you're going to be playing for the state title, you're going to need your own bed." I put up a half-hearted argument, but I was glad to get my room back.

But that didn't mean I was able to sleep. For the second straight night, I lay staring at the ceiling, thinking. I thought about Monica and the wolf masks and the hands grabbing and tearing at her; about my mother hugging me and my father saying how much he trusted me; about Josh's slider and what Hernandes had said in the shower.

But always my mind came back to Detective Langford and one thing she had said: *You shape your own world.*

▪ 8 ▪

What I needed was time — time to think things through, to get a grip on what to do. But time was one thing I didn't have. Everything was racing along, carrying me with it whether I was ready or not. The first game of the state tournament was Thursday at three o'clock in Tacoma.

There was a pep rally last period on Wednesday. The baseball team sat down on the floor of the gym while the pep team did flips and the band blared the fight song. It felt strange sitting there with everybody staring down at us. My head was pounding from the music and from lack of sleep.

Eventually Coach Wheatley walked to the microphone. "On behalf of the team," he said, looking up into the stands, "I'd like to thank you for the support you've given us this year. Now it's our turn to give something back to you." He reached under the podium, retrieved a gleaming silver trophy and held it high above his head. He read the inscription: "Crown Hill Vikings — Metro Region Champions!"

The place went nuts. Kids stomped and screamed.

Chanting started: "Take the State! Take the State! Take the State!"

Wheatley held up his hand for quiet. "I know you love us," he joked. "But I also know you want to go home on time. So let me move on." The place quieted, and he continued. "Individual awards don't mean a whole heck of a lot if a team doesn't do well, but when a team does well, then it's a pleasure to give them out. This year it is a pleasure. The trophy for Most Valuable Player goes to . . . Josh Daniels!"

Again the gym exploded. Kids rose to their feet; they stomped; they whistled. Josh strode to the podium, shook Coach Wheatley's hand, and took the trophy. A new chant started: "Daniels! Daniels! Daniels!" Josh thrust his trophy into the air in rhythm.

"The coaches decide the MVP award," Wheatley went on. "But this next trophy is voted by the players. It goes to a young man who was the last player to make the team. I penciled his name in only when I'd counted the uniforms and was sure I had enough. He doesn't have big numbers, but he's got a big heart. Our Most Inspirational Player is Ryan Ward."

I was so stunned that even after I heard my name I didn't move. Garrett Curtis had to nudge me to get me up to the podium. But once Coach Wheatley put that trophy in my hand, once I grasped it tight, waves of pleasure, of excitement, rolled through my body. I looked to my teammates and they were all smiling and clapping for me. "Ward! Ward! Ward!" was the chant that was coming down from the rafters. Josh came over to me, put his arm around my shoulder, and the two of us raised our trophies into the air together.

Coach Cliff came up, put his hand out to me. "Congratulations," he said. "Congratulations."

Mr. Haskin took over the assembly. The baseball team moved to the first few rows of the bleachers as he read off all the other prizes and awards. Chess Club, Math Club, Cheerleaders, Choir. On and on he went. I wasn't listening. I was holding that gleaming trophy so tightly my knuckles were white.

"Finally," Haskin said, and when I heard that word I came back to attention, "this year, for the first time in the history of our school, a Crown Hill High student has been named the *Seattle Times* High School Student of the Year. Her achievement is really quite remarkable. So even though she's not here today, let's have a round of applause for Monica Roby."

■ 9 ■

I had another bad practice that afternoon, only this time Coach Wheatley was there to notice. "Something wrong with you, Ward?" he asked after the third routine throw home skipped by me to the backstop.

"I'm okay," I replied. "I just haven't been sleeping."

"Well, you look terrible and you're playing worse.

Go home and get some shuteye. I want you ready to-morrow."

I argued, but just a little. The prospect of lying down, of actually sleeping, seemed wonderful.

I didn't need to shower; I'd hardly worked up a sweat. I changed out of my cleats and went straight home. My parents would both be at work. I could go to my room and sleep, and not think about anything.

But I'd forgotten about Grandpa Kevin. When I opened my front door he was there, sitting in the big easy chair, reading a book. I think I startled him as much as he startled me.

"No practice?" he said, when he'd recovered himself.

"No," I said. "I mean yes. Actually I'm not feeling real hot, so Coach sent me home."

He smiled. "Well, that was smart of him. You don't look one hundred percent to me either. You're no good to the team sick."

"I'm fine," I said. "I'm just tired. I think I'll try to get some shuteye."

I crossed the room and had one foot on the staircase when his voice stopped me.

"Ryan, is there anything you want to talk about?"

My face went red. "No, nothing."

"Because if there's something you couldn't tell your parents or that policewoman, you might try me. I'm not such a bad listener. And I've been alive a few years, too, so nothing much shocks me."

"There's nothing, Grandpa."

He sort of winked at me, and I knew he knew I was

212

lying. I felt like a little kid who'd been caught stealing quarters. "Get some sleep, then. And if you do want to talk sometime, I'll be here."

Upstairs in my room I dropped onto my bed, but I still couldn't sleep. I felt like my head was going to explode. I didn't want to have to look at anybody or talk to anybody or do anything. I wanted everything to be over with — the baseball season, the school year, everything.

My parents came home, and somehow I made it through dinner. My mother helped. She'd been to an open house up in the Highlands, the fanciest neighborhood in Seattle, and she went on and on about all the rooms and the view of the Puget Sound and the gardens.

Once dinner was over, I went back upstairs to my room. I had homework, so I unpacked my school bag. Down at the bottom I found my trophy. I held it in my hand, thinking how happy it would make my mother and father and grandfather to see it. But I couldn't bring it down to them. I ended up shoving it into a bottom drawer under some shirts I never wear.

I sat at my desk and looked at my chemistry book for about five minutes. Then I closed it and went downstairs. My parents and Grandpa Kevin were watching television.

"I'm going to go see Josh," I said as I pulled on my shoes. "Go over our game plan for tomorrow."

"Don't be out too late," my mother said.

* * *

When Josh saw me at his front door, his body flinched. But he gave me his usual smile. "You okay?" he asked. "I was worried when I saw you leave practice. I need you tomorrow, you know."

I shrugged. "I know. And I'll be okay. Look, can we go someplace and talk."

"Sure," he said. "For a while. But I've got stuff to do."

We ended up sitting on the stairs in front of the Community Center, sipping Cokes we'd bought inside the building.

"I can't keep doing this," I said. "Maybe you can, but I can't."

"What are you talking about?" he asked.

"Haskin, the police, my grandfather, my parents. I'm sick of lying to them, Josh. I can't look anybody in the eye. I can't even look you in the eye."

He took a long swig of his Coke, wiped his mouth. "Listen, Ryan, I know how you feel. I've gone through the same thing. Haskin grilled me. The police have been over, talking to me and my mother and my old man. Even Wheatley pulled me in. But it's over, buddy. They're done. There's nothing more they can say or do. It's like I told you right at the start. They can't prove anything."

We both were silent as two girls walked by us, up the stairs, and into the Community Center.

"Unless somebody tells them," I said once the girls were gone.

He smiled. "Who would tell them? I'm not going to. And —" He stopped. "You're not thinking of talking, are you? That's not what this is all about, is it?"

I sucked in some air. "I don't know, Josh. I really don't know what I'm going to do."

I could see the astonishment in his face. "I can't believe I'm hearing this. You're thinking of selling me out for Monica Roby?"

I felt my whole body sag. "It's not for Monica Roby," I said, trying to explain. "And I don't want to sell you out. It's . . . it's . . ."

"It's what?" he interrupted. "What? Tell me."

I'd thought that talking to him would help me pull my thoughts together, but it hadn't. "Nothing feels right anymore, Josh," was all I could manage.

He was quiet for a long time. "Okay. I shouldn't have done it," he finally said. "It was stupid. I should have just left her alone. But it's not like I really hurt her or anything. She's still alive. She's still winning her little prizes. Besides, it's done and there's no undoing it. What matters is what's ahead of us. The games are what matter. Winning the championship is what matters. You know that."

I ran my hand through my hair. "But that's just it. I *don't* know it. Or at least I'm not sure about it."

"Come on, Ryan," he said, almost pleading. "What are you talking about? We're a team, you and me. Setting a batter up with fastballs inside, then striking him out with the slider away. I love doing that, and I want to keep doing it, all the way to the end. I can't believe you feel any different."

I sat thinking for a while. "I do want to keep doing it," I said at last. "More than anything in the world."

He stood. "Okay then. So it's settled. We'll just play

ball like always." He looked at his watch. "I've got to get back now. But I'll see you tomorrow at school."

He started off, but before he'd gone far I called to him. "Josh," I said, "who was the other guy with you?"

He started to answer, then checked himself. "I promised I wouldn't tell anyone." He let those words hang in the air a moment, then he walked away.

It was simple when Josh was on the pitcher's mound firing the ball to me, overwhelming batter after batter. On the diamond, the rules are all laid out, and there is a rule for everything. I wished it were that simple everywhere.

I went home. I was afraid I wouldn't be able to sleep, but I dropped off right away. I was so tired my body just gave out.

▪ 10 ▪

Thursday. Game day.

I got up late, which made everything a rush. As I picked at my breakfast, my mother complained about the travel arrangements for the game. "I don't see why you can't just get in the car with us and go to the game."

"I've told you, Mother. Coach Wheatley wants the team all together."

"And I want our family all together," she snapped.

"There's nothing I can do about it," I said, heading for the door.

"Oh, I know," she answered, her voice gentler. Then she gave me a kiss on the forehead. "I'm just nervous. I'm glad you were able to sleep last night. I didn't."

The kids at Crown Hill were nervous too. The halls buzzed with baseball talk. Guys patted me on the back and wished me luck. "Go get 'em!" they said.

"You bet," I answered.

The school was on a half-day schedule so people could make it to Tacoma for the game. I thought even the half day would drag, but there was so much tension that the first three classes flew by. I had no time to plan; no time to think.

Then came Ms. Hurley's class. I still wasn't used to Monica's not being there. And that day, with the game just hours away, her empty chair seemed even more empty.

The other teachers had gone easy, figuring that nobody was up for studying. But Ms. Hurley tried to run a normal class. We were supposed to discuss a story I hadn't read. Actually, it seemed as though nobody had read it. As the minutes ticked by, I could feel Ms. Hurley's growing frustration. I wanted to help her out, but there was nothing I could do. When the bell finally rang it was like being released from prison.

Only I wasn't released. "Could you stay a minute, Ryan?" she asked, and from the way she said it I knew it had to do with Monica. Josh knew it too. He looked over at me as he left, a question in his eyes.

Once we were alone, Ms. Hurley took a deep breath and then began. "I've been wanting to tell you how much I appreciate what you did for Monica. I'm sure you know she's special to me."

I nodded.

She went on. "There's something else I've been wanting to ask. Something a little harder." She fiddled with a pencil in her hand. "You don't think Josh was involved, do you? Because if he was I'd feel —"

"It wasn't Josh," I said, cutting her off.

"How can you be so sure?" she asked, surprised by my certainty. "I thought they were wearing masks."

"I'm sure," I said. "I'm absolutely positive it wasn't him."

She sighed. "Well, that's a load off my mind. I kept thinking that maybe something had happened in class that . . ."

"It wasn't Josh," I repeated, interrupting again.

"Good," she said. "Good."

I looked up at the clock. "Ms. Hurley, I'm supposed to be . . ."

"I'm sorry, Ryan. You go." I headed for the door. "And good luck!"

I hurried down the hall and away from that classroom. I was just starting to breathe normally again when I pushed open the door that led out of the building to the gym. There, in the doorway, was Josh.

"What was that all about?" he demanded.

"What was it about?" I said, my frustration boiling over at last. "I'll tell you what it was about. It was about me covering for you, that's what it was about. That's what everything is about these days, isn't it? And you know what else, Josh? You know what else? I shouldn't be doing it. And you shouldn't be making me do it."

He stepped back, stunned. Right then Brandon Ruben called out to us. "Coach sent me looking for you two. We've got a game today, in case you forgot. You guys coming, or you got something better to do?"

"We're coming," Josh managed. "We're coming."

In the parking lot the bus started up, a big cloud of black smoke coming out of its exhaust pipe. I walked down the steps and headed toward it. Josh followed behind.

▪ 11 ▪

Cheney Stadium is the home of the Tacoma Rainiers, the Mariners' Triple-A club. Before that the Oakland Athletics ran the team, and before them the San Francisco Giants. Mark McGwire and José Canseco started at Cheney, and so did Juan Marichal and Willie McCovey. And besides them there must have been hundreds of guys who didn't make it, guys you've never heard of, who weren't quite good enough to take that final step into the major leagues.

I felt that history as I dressed, felt it in the air around

me. The adrenaline started flowing through me, pumping me up. I tried to block out everything negative. *Baseball*, I told myself, *just think about baseball. Nothing but baseball.* There'll be time after the game to sort out the other things.

Before we took the field, Coach Cliff gave a little speech, and when he finished the guys let out a roar, a roar of pure desire. They wanted it. And I wanted it too.

I was swept along with them up the runway and onto the field. Once I was on the diamond, I fell into my normal pre-game routine — a little running, a little batting practice, some infield.

There were probably a thousand people at the game, way more than what we had for any regular season game. My father, mother, and grandfather came right down to the backstop. They called to me, huge smiles on their faces, and I waved. "Go get 'em!" my father shouted.

When it was Chehalis's turn to take batting practice, I warmed Josh up along the sideline. We were totally out of sync off the field, but on the field we fell right into our regular rhythm. It was throw and catch, throw and catch, throw and catch. I knew his pitches like I knew myself.

Finally it was game time. We were the home team, and our fans rose and cheered as we took the field. I settled in behind home plate and looked out at Josh and the other guys. The outfield grass was lush and green, the dirt infield immaculately raked. It was by far the best field I've ever played on.

The ump yelled, "Play ball!" Josh took his final warm-up toss. I fired the ball down to second. It went around the horn and came back to him.

▪ 12 ▪

Playing the game was a relief. There was no time to think. I had a job to do, and I did it.

Josh came out pumped — too pumped. His pitches had velocity and movement — they exploded into my mitt. But they were nowhere near the plate. I kept holding my mitt down, trying to settle him, but he walked the first two hitters on ten pitches.

I called time and went out to the mound. I don't remember what I said. I'm sure he paid no attention anyway. I just wanted to slow him down. Back behind the plate I called for a changeup. He shook me off, wanting to stay with that live fastball. I kept flashing changeup until he gave in.

It was the right pitch, too. The Chehalis hitter lunged at the ball, sending a pop fly to short right field for what should have been an easy out. But Josh wasn't the only guy on our team who was tight. Santos took two steps back, then sprinted in, overrunning the ball. At the last second he reached back for it. He almost caught it, too, but the ball hit off the heel of his glove and trickled toward short center. By the time he ran it down, one run had scored and Chehalis had guys at second and third.

In some baseball games the key moment comes in the first inning. This was one of those games. Our fans were way back in their seats, hunched in fear. The Chehalis fans were up cheering, hoping for a clutch hit that would open the flood gates. Their cleanup batter, a big burly guy with a long swing and a thick mustache, stepped in.

The minute I saw that long swing, I knew that if Josh could get himself under control, we could strike the guy out. I called for a fastball and put my mitt over the inside half of the plate. Josh nodded, and the instant I saw his eyes I knew the nervousness was gone, that he was focused. He stretched, and then hit my target with a blazing fastball. "Strike one!" the umpire called. I called for another fastball, this time down and away. Again Josh hit the target exactly. "Strike two!" the umpire called.

The Chehalis fans booed. The mustached guy glared at the umpire. But we had him. I called for the slider. The guy swung over the top, and we had our first out.

The number five hitter was another big guy who looked like a free swinger. I figured he'd be looking for a fastball, so I started him off with a change that he fouled to right. Then came more off-speed stuff, a curve that nipped the inside corner for the second strike. Josh wasted another curve a foot outside, then came in with the heater on the fists. The guy swung, but his timing was so far off, the ball was in my glove before he got around.

Two down.

The next batter was different. He was medium-sized; he choked way up on the bat; and his swing was compact. I moved the outfielders in a few steps.

Josh came with a fastball, and the guy bounced a two-hopper to Curtis at third. Easy as pie. Or it should have been.

Curtis fielded the ball okay, but his throw short-hopped Combs and bounded down the right field line. The lead runner scored easily, but Santos charged the ball quickly and fired toward home. I peeked up the third base line and saw the runner thundering toward me. It was going to be a close play, and I was going to take a hit.

I blocked home with my left leg, willing the ball to come faster, faster. I felt the runner on me as I caught the ball. I spun to make the tag, but I didn't get all the way around. The next thing I knew I was flat on my back. The ball was on the ground next to me; the ump was yelling, "Safe!" and my right hand felt strangely warm. I'd been spiked. The flesh was torn from my wrist to my ring finger.

Time was called and some doctor cleaned out the cut and bandaged it. I hustled back out to a round of applause from everybody in the stands. Josh got the next batter on a comebacker and the inning was finally over. But we were down 3–0.

Falling behind right away is about the worst thing that can happen to a team in a big game. It doubles the pressure you already feel, and it eases the pressure on your opponent. The Chehalis pitcher, a rangy left-hander with long stringy blond hair, came out throwing strikes, and the Chehalis fielders made the plays behind him. We went down one-two-three.

In the second our butterflies were gone, and we played like the team we really were. Josh was around the plate with every pitch, and I stole a couple of strikes for him by framing his pitches just right. Ruben made a nice play on the one ball that was hit, a grounder up the middle that he cut off before it slithered into center, and it was Chehalis that went in order.

After that the game raced along. Their lefty was tough. He had a herky-jerky motion that made it hard to pick up the ball. I struck out in the third — my hand ached on every swing — and it wasn't until the fourth — when Chang blooped a double down the right field line — that we got our first hit.

All along I'd assumed we'd win, that Josh was invincible, unbeatable. That's how he'd been all year; that's how he'd always seemed to me. But somewhere in the middle of that game I realized we could lose, and when I did, I felt a sudden panic.

I popped up to lead off the sixth. But Brandon Ruben stroked a triple down the line in left and scored on a single by Van Tassel, cutting the Chehalis lead to 3–1. My heart started pumping, feeling a rally coming, but Curtis struck out, and Chang hit a comebacker to the mound. That one run was all we got.

Josh was tired, and he was losing, but he didn't let down. There was nothing second-rate about him on the baseball diamond. His fastball was gone, so he mixed speeds — curves and sliders and changeups. The Chehalis guys were no match for him. Two little ground outs and a strikeout. The top of the seventh was over. We were down to our final three outs.

Back on the bench I took off my shin guards and my chest protector. As I did, it struck me that I might never wear them again. I'd been a catcher for only one year, but it seemed like that's what I was somehow, a catcher, and laying my gear in a pile by the bench felt a little bit like burying myself.

I was scheduled to bat fifth in the inning. I grabbed my bat and sat holding it, listening to the thin cheers of the guys around me. "We can do it!" . . . "Let's get this guy!" There was more noise than hope.

Dillon Combs led off. He took the first two pitches for balls, and then got a good swing on a fastball, lifting a towering fly ball to deep center. The guys jumped up and cheered their heads off. If we'd been at Woodland Park, the ball would have been gone. But at Cheney the Chehalis outfielder had all day to settle under it for the first out.

Andy Bayne was next. He was first-pitch swinging, and he hit a grounder to second and was thrown out easily.

As Carlos Hernandes stepped in, the Chehalis fans rose, clapping their hands rhythmically, anticipating that final out. I couldn't watch, but I couldn't keep from watching. My eyes went up and down between the cement floor of the dugout and the field.

The lefty went into his wind-up, and delivered. It was

a fastball, and in his excitement he overthrew it. The ball sailed up and in, catching Hernandes in the back. Carlos went down in pain, but on our bench we cheered. We had a little life, and my pulse quickened. If Santos got on, it would be up to me.

Bethel stepped to the plate as I stepped to the on-deck circle. The lefty stretched, checked Hernandes at first, and delivered a fastball that was two feet outside. The catcher tossed the ball back. The lefty caught it, stretched his arm out, leaned forward with his hands on his knees.

He was done. Just like that, he was on empty. You could see it in his face, in his every motion. Santos sensed it too, and dug in. The next pitch was nothing. I don't know if it was supposed to be a fastball or a curve or a changeup. Bethel was all over it though, ripping a line drive into right center field. Hernandes raced to third and Santos pulled into second standing up. It was my turn. It was all coming to me.

I wasn't going to face the lefty, though. The Chehalis coach came slowly walking out of the dugout, his eyes on the ground. I knew he had a hook with him, so my eyes went down to the bullpen where a big right-hander was warming up furiously.

The coach talked for a while, then motioned down to the right-hander. The fans applauded the lefty as he made his way off the diamond, and I stepped aside and took some practice swings as the right-hander came to the mound and took his warm-up tosses.

I didn't make it obvious, but I watched those warm-up

throws. He was good. His fastball had pop and it had some movement too. It was going to be a tough at-bat.

Just before I stepped in, the crowd, Chehalis fans and Crown Hill fans alike, rose to their feet and cheered. They were cheering for their team, but even if they didn't realize it they were cheering for the game of baseball too, for the greatness of moments like this one. Chills ran up and down my spine and out over my whole body.

The right-hander completed his warm-ups. I looked down to Wheatley. No signs at all. "Get a good pitch to hit," he called to me. My heart was thumping so loud it felt like somebody was playing the drums inside me. I picked up some dirt and rubbed it in my gloves. Then I took a deep breath and stepped in.

I don't think I could have swung at the first pitch even if the guy had lobbed it up to me. I was that nervous. As it was, he missed with a fastball outside. I was ready for the second pitch, but it was another fastball way outside. I stepped out and took a couple of deep breaths. *Okay, I told myself, if it's up in the strike zone and out over the plate, take it right back up the middle. Otherwise, let it go.*

The right-hander stretched and delivered. A fastball in on my hands. I almost hacked at it, but I didn't pull the trigger. "Strike one!" the ump yelled.

But that was okay. I was still ahead in the count.

Again he stretched and delivered. And there it was — a fastball out over the plate, right where I was looking for it. I reached out and got it, a smooth stroke on top of the ball. I watched it slither right back up the center of the diamond and into center field for a base hit. Santos scored, Curtis scored — and we were tied.

I don't know why Wheatley didn't pull me for a pinch runner. I was the slowest guy on the team and I was the potential winning run. The only thing I can figure is that he was so excited he forgot.

I led a few steps off as Brandon Ruben stepped to the plate. Ruben took a ball, then a strike. That's when I felt something crawling on my skin. I looked at my hand and saw that blood was pouring from my cut. I almost called time, but I'm glad I didn't, because Brandon ripped the next pitch into right center field. With two outs I was off on contact, and as I hit second base I looked for Wheatley. His arm was going like a windmill in a storm. He was going to try to score me. I kept under control — short steps, but lots of them. I hit the corner of third base in stride and headed for home.

I felt like I was running forever, like my feet were in sand, in mud. But however long it took me, the throw from the outfield took one tenth of one second more. I slid in under the catcher's tag. The umpire's arms went out.

Safe!

We'd won 4–3!

The guys mobbed me; they lifted me up and carried me off the field. Riding high like that, way up on their shoulders, I grinned so hard my cheeks hurt.

Finally they put me down, and still grinning, I headed to the locker room. Josh came up next to me. "You think this is good," he said, "just imagine what winning the title will be like. It'll make everything else go away. You wait and see."

Right then, right when I was on top of the world, I finally knew what I had to do. Not because I thought he was wrong, but because I was afraid he was right.

▪ 13 ▪

I called as soon as I got home. My hand was shaking so much it was hard to punch in the number. I was using the upstairs phone, and I kept thinking somebody would hear me. They'd have to know sometime, but I didn't want them to know just yet.

I asked for Detective Langford, but the voice on the other end said she wasn't in. "Give me your name and number and I'll have her call you."

I swallowed, and gave my name. "I'd like to talk to her right away," I added.

"Is this an emergency?" the voice asked.

I told him I wasn't sure.

His voice was gruff. "Is somebody going to die if she doesn't call you back in the next five minutes?"

"No," I answered.

"Then she'll call you tomorrow morning."

Before I could say another word, he hung up.

I sat there holding the dead telephone, my whole body

numb. Then I almost laughed out loud. You get it in your head that what's happening to you is the most important thing in the world. I had this stupid movie vision of Detective Langford waiting at the station for my call. She'd hear my voice and she'd rush out to her car and race over to get my statement. What an idiot I was! She must have hundreds of cases to worry about — and every one was probably more serious than what Josh had done! She might have forgotten all about it. I felt like a fool, an absolute fool.

Still, all that evening I was jumpy, and the three or four times the phone rang I popped up to get it. None of the callers was Officer Langford.

Around nine o'clock Grandpa Kevin came upstairs and knocked on my door. I really didn't want to talk to anybody. Had he been my mother or father I would have told him that straight out, but I couldn't say it to him.

"You got a minute?"

"Sure," I said, but he must have heard the doubt in my voice.

"I won't be long. I know you've got things on your mind."

"That's okay. What is it?"

"I just wanted you to know you're a terrific catcher."

I shrugged. "When you've got a pitcher like Josh Daniels —"

He didn't let me finish. "When you've got a pitcher like Josh, it's harder. He's out there on the black all the time, and you've got to frame the ball just right, or the umpire won't give you the call. Remember, I was a catcher too. I know the game." He paused. "You're a good ball player, the kind of ball player I'd like to think I was."

"Thanks, Grandpa," I said softly.

He stood. "Well, that's all I wanted to say." He headed to the door.

I had a sudden desire to tell him everything. "Grandpa Kevin," I said as he stood in the doorway.

He turned back to me. "Yes, Ryan?"

I could feel the kindness in his soft gray eyes. Too much kindness. "Thanks again for the gear and for your help and everything."

"Sure, Ryan. It's been my pleasure. Watching you play has given me a chance to relive a part of my own life."

I felt numb walking to school the next morning. It was hard to believe that it was all going to be over soon. I was sure something would happen first period, but nothing did. Second period came and went. Still nothing. I wondered if the message had gotten lost, if I should call again. Then, during the passing period, Mr. Phelps tapped me on the shoulder. "Mr. Haskin wants you in his office." I must have looked blank. "Did you hear me?"

"Yeah," I said. "I heard you."

I could hear voices as I tapped on Haskin's door, so I knew he wasn't alone. But I didn't expect what I got when I opened the door.

Everyone was there. Mr. Haskin, Detective Langford,

Coach Wheatley, Mr. and Mrs. Roby. I felt cold suddenly, looking at them.

"Sit down, Ryan," Mr. Haskin said, nodding toward a chair right in the middle of the room.

I sat. For a long moment no one said anything. Then Detective Langford took out her yellow notebook and flipped to a clean page. "I believe you have some information you'd like to share."

When I finished, they took turns saying all the expected things: "We're glad you came forward." . . . "We know this took courage."

But I was nobody's hero anymore. I was just another confused kid who didn't know what he was doing. I didn't leave anything out, but they didn't believe me, at least not one hundred percent. I could see the mistrust in their eyes, especially in Mr. and Mrs. Roby's.

"You can go back to class," Mr. Haskin said. "You're all done for now."

But I wasn't done. Coming out of Haskin's office, I knew there was something else I had to do. I had to be the one to tell Josh. I figured they'd call him to the office right away. He had history in Room 24, so I hung out at the end of the twenty-wing hallway.

I wasn't there more than a minute when a door opened and he came out. When he saw me, the color drained out of him. "You did it, didn't you? You sold me out."

"I told them the truth, Josh."

He looked away from me for an instant, then pounded

his fist hard against one of the lockers. The noise was like a gunshot. I jumped a little. He looked back at me. "You could have been part of a championship team, you know. All you had to do was keep your mouth shut. Now it's gone. All of it. Not just for you, but for everybody. You trashed it for nothing."

He stared at me for a long moment. Then he walked by me toward the office. I watched him until he'd gone around the corner and out of sight.

· 14 ·

I don't know when it hit me that the baseball season wasn't over, that I had practice that afternoon and a game on Saturday. When it did, I went lightheaded. For a second I thought about quitting the team, about walking away from it all. I'd faced Josh, but I wasn't sure I had it in me to face the rest of the team. I only thought that way for a second, though. You start something, you finish it.

Word gets around a school fast. By lunch time Santos and Ruben were on me, asking me where Josh was and what I'd told the police.

"I don't want to talk about it," I said.

"What's that supposed to mean?" Ruben snapped.

"It means I don't have anything to say."

They glared at me, their mouths open in disbelief. But finally they gave up and walked away.

It only got worse. Dressing for practice after school, all the guys were talking about Josh, how he'd been called out of class and hadn't come back. Wilkerson said that someone told him they saw a police car drive off with Josh in the back seat. Bayne said that wasn't true, that Josh's parents had come and gotten him. It seemed like everybody knew something.

"Ryan knows what's really going on," Santos said loudly, "only he's not saying."

In a flash, all eyes were on me. I sat up straight and looked around the room, looked at every one of them.

"That's right," I said. "I'm not." Then I pulled my shoelaces tight, double-knotted them, grabbed my mitt, and headed outside.

When I took the field I had nobody to warm up with. I remembered that first day of tryouts, how the exact same thing had happened, and how Josh had come over and rescued me. Only it wasn't the same thing, it wasn't the same thing at all, because now I didn't need rescuing.

I stretched my legs and my back, then ran in place for a few minutes. I'd barely broken a sweat when Wheatley came out of the coach's office. He blew his whistle and motioned for us to come forward. His face was grim and he stood almost at attention.

He said what I knew he'd say. Josh had been suspended from the team for assaulting a female student. If anybody else was involved, he wanted that person to come forward. Guys looked around at one another, wondering who it might be.

"I'm not going to pretend that losing Josh isn't a blow to our team," Wheatley went on. "We all know what kind of pitcher he is, how much he has meant to us. But we can't quit. Starting right now, with today's practice, each and every one of us is going to have to dig a little deeper, give a little more. So let's get out there and do it."

A couple of guys cheered then. But most were too stunned to do anything but stand. It wasn't until Wheatley strode toward the center of the diamond that everyone moved.

That practice wasn't good. Not for me, not for anyone. The fielding was sloppy and the hitting was bad. Guys kept forming into clumps of two or three. They'd talk behind their gloves and kick at the ground until either Wheatley or Cliff would yell at them and get them shagging balls or running in the outfield. The two hours seemed like ten.

In the locker room afterward I could feel Ruben's eyes on me, and Chang's, and Santos's, and other guys'. They knew what I'd done. I don't know how they knew, but they knew. I could feel their anger.

I did everything at my normal pace. If anything I took longer. I'd been hiding for too long, and I was done with it. Not one of those guys said a word to me. Not one. When I looked them in the eye, they were the ones who looked down and away. And when I left the locker room, Ruben moved aside to let me pass.

My work wasn't over, either. I still had to tell my parents and Grandpa Kevin. Walking home I thought about waiting until after dinner, or maybe even until the next morning. But I wanted to get everything over with. I *had* to get everything over with. So as soon as I stepped through my front door, I told them the truth.

By the time I finished, my father's face was beet red. "I can't believe you let me say those things to Officer Langford! I can't believe you sat there and let me make an idiot of myself!"

"I'm sorry," I said.

That made him angrier. "Sorry! You're sorry. Well, that's just great."

My mom came to my defense. "The important thing is that in the end he told the truth."

My father scowled. "Yeah? Well, it would have been nice if he'd told the truth in the beginning." He stared at me long and hard. "I'll call Officer Langford tomorrow and apologize," he said at last. Then he turned and went into the kitchen.

My mother followed him, leaving me alone with Grandpa Kevin. I sank back into the sofa, exhausted. For a while neither of us said anything. Then I took a deep breath and exhaled. "I've really made a mess of things, haven't I?"

He shrugged. I think he might have even smiled. "Don't be so hard on yourself. Everybody makes a mess sometimes. At least you're trying to clean yours up."

After dinner I went straight to my room, lay on my bed, closed my eyes, and tried to relax. The hardest part was over. I'd done it and I'd never have to do it again.

But instead of feeling better, I felt worse. Waves of panic swept over me. I wanted desperately to go back and undo everything. Then I pulled myself together. I told myself I'd done the right thing, the only thing. The panic passed, only to come back again minutes later.

▪ 15 ▪

It took me forever to fall asleep and stay asleep, which actually worked out. The game was at noon Saturday. I woke up so late that by the time I'd finished eating breakfast it was time to go.

My father drove me to the Crown Hill parking lot, where the team bus was waiting. In the car I could feel him wanting to say something, but he never did. Just before I got out, he reached over and rubbed the top of my head. "I'll be cheering for you today."

The locker room of the gym was open. I went inside, grabbed my equipment bag, then returned to the parking lot. The big yellow bus was sitting there, empty. All the guys were standing around outside, talking.

I hung back, off by myself, until Wheatley called out that it was time to go. Then I was the first to get on. I felt shaky and hot, as though I had a fever, and I was glad to be able to sit down.

I took a seat about halfway back. As the other guys boarded, I stared out the window. The seat next to me was empty, and I figured it would stay empty.

But I was wrong about that. As the engine of the bus started up, Chris Selin slid in next to me. "You mind if I sit here?" he asked.

"No," I said, hoping my voice sounded normal. "Not at all." Then we were off, bumping down Sixty-fifth toward the freeway.

The bus was real quiet. Some guys talked, but only in whispers, as if we were all headed to a funeral.

It wasn't until we reached Boeing Field that Selin spoke. First it was nothing stuff. The weather, Cheney Stadium, graduation. But it felt good to know there was somebody on the team who would talk to me, even if it was about nothing.

"Let me take a look at your hands," Selin said as we took the freeway exit that led to Cheney Stadium.

It was such a strange, unexpected request that I wasn't sure I'd heard him right. "My hands?"

"Yeah. Let me see them."

I held them out in front of me. It was the first time I'd looked closely at them in months, and what I saw startled me. The palm and all the fingers on my left hand were swollen and slightly blue. On my right hand two of my knuckles were huge, almost twice their normal size. A long scab ran across the back of my hand, and the skin under three of my fingernails was deep purple. My little finger seemed bent, as though I'd broken it.

"They're even worse than mine," Selin said, holding his out for me to see.

"I don't know," I said, looking at all the swelling. "Yours are pretty ugly too."

We both stared at our hands for a minute. Then Selin's voice went serious. "A lot of guys on this bus think you let us down. I'm not one of them. I know what you did for us this year. And I know what you did for Josh, even if he doesn't. It's right there, in those hands. And in your sore knees and your stiff ankles. It was Josh who let us down, not you. That's why no one's ever going to say a bad word about you in front of me and get away with it."

When he finished, both of us sat completely still for a moment. I'm not sure what I would have said if he'd stayed. I'd like to think I would have thanked him, but I'll never know, because he stood and quickly moved to an empty seat at the back of the bus.

It's easy to say that you don't care what the world thinks of you, that you live only for yourself. It sounds strong and tough, and like a man. But there are times when you need a good word from somebody. For me that was one of those times. I didn't feel good when I got off the bus, but I felt better than I had. I owe that to Chris Selin.

I don't know how to describe the game. It was as if we were there, but we weren't there. From the start Reule couldn't get the ball over the plate. He fell behind every batter, and then he'd have to come in with some fat pitch down the heart of the plate. The Yakima hitters pounded base hits to all corners of the park. But it wasn't just Reule; it was everybody. We made two errors in the first and two more in the second. By the third we were down 8–0. Wheatley had no choice but to bring in Wilkerson, and then Smith. Nothing worked. For them it was like batting practice. For us it was a long nightmare that wouldn't end. Wheatley sent me up as a pinch hitter in the seventh. It was a nice thing to do. It let me know he wasn't holding anything against me. I wanted to pay him back with a solid hit somewhere, but I struck out on a curve that bounced up to the plate. The final score was 14–2.

In the clubhouse afterwards Wheatley gave a little speech. He told us we had nothing to be ashamed of, and he thanked us for giving him a great ride. Then he said we could go home with our parents if we wanted. I think just about everybody did. An hour bus ride together after getting pasted didn't sound like much of a trip.

My parents and Grandpa Kevin were waiting just outside the gate. "I'm sorry," my mom said, and she gave me a hug. Then we walked together to the car. I got in and pulled the door closed.

The season was over.

▪ 16 ▪

For the next couple of days I kept my eye on Josh's house. Sometime or other, I'd have to talk to him again, and I wanted to get it over with. At night I'd see a light in his window, so I knew he was there. But during the day he must have been lying low, because he was never in front of his house or at the Community Center or anywhere.

After school on Wednesday, Officer Langford called. "It's all settled. Josh has agreed to do forty hours of community service and to take an anger-management class. He could have had the time reduced to twenty hours if he'd identified the other boy, but he wouldn't."

I told my mom and dad that evening at dinner. "That's it?" my mom asked.

"That's it," I answered. For a long moment nobody said anything. I think my parents were feeling the same way I was. What Josh got didn't seem wrong, yet somehow it didn't seem right either. The only good thing was that that part was over.

After dinner I went to my room. I was there ten minutes or so when my dad came up. "You got a minute?"

"Sure," I said.

He turned my desk chair around and sat in it backwards. "I'm not proud of the way I acted," he said. "I'm not proud at all."

"What do you mean?" I asked.

"The way I got angry. It wasn't right."

"Forget it," I said. "Besides, you had reason to be mad."

He shook his head. "No. Telling the truth cost you a lot. I should have been very proud of you." He paused. "I am now, you know."

"No," I said. "I didn't know."

He stood, went to my door, and opened it. Then he

looked back to me. "I told you that you had greatness in you, didn't I?"

He closed the door quickly and escaped before I could answer. I sat there feeling a familiar irritation with him, and then I found myself smiling. It was the first time in a long time anything had struck me as funny.

I felt okay about what I'd done. I could look people in the eye again. But my father was probably the only person in the world who would call what I had done great.

Thursday night was graduation. The ceremony was held at the Seattle Arena. I sat on a metal folding chair on the floor while my parents and my grandfather looked down at me from the rafters. I checked over the program. Josh was listed, but he wasn't there. I don't know whether he wasn't allowed to graduate with the class, or whether he just didn't want to.

The valedictorian was Monica Roby. She'd never come back to school after Josh's attack, so I figured she wouldn't be at graduation either. But I figured wrong. She gave a speech all right. Did she ever! It was pure Monica Roby. She quoted Shakespeare and Hemingway, her voice rising and falling dramatically. The applause when she finished was loud and long.

There were a few more speeches, and then the reading of the names. They went in alphabetical order, so I was way at the end of the list, as usual. It was boring watching everybody else tramp across the stage. But when it was my turn, my heart was pounding.

The graduation gowns were rented, but we got to keep

our mortarboards. That night, in my room, I sat on my bed fiddling with the tassel for a while, thinking about Monica and Josh and all that had happened. Finally I tossed it into a corner, turned out the light, and went to sleep.

When I got up on Friday morning my father was at work, but my mother and grandfather were sitting at the kitchen table. We talked a little about the night before, then I flipped through the sports pages while I ate my cereal.

I'd taken about two bites when I stopped cold. Josh's face was staring out at me from the newspaper. I quickly read the article. Major league baseball had held its June draft. He'd been the sixteenth player selected, chosen in the first round by the Colorado Rockies. The article said his signing bonus would probably be between one and two million dollars.

My face must have gone pale. "Is something wrong?" my grandfather said.

I slid the article toward him. My mother read it, too, leaning over his shoulder. She put her hand to her mouth, but Grandpa Kevin just nodded his head up and down as he read. "Well, what do you know?" he said. "What do you know?" From what I saw, the kid had great stuff. He might just make it if he can get his head screwed on right."

"Yeah," I agreed. "He might."

Grandpa Kevin put the newspaper down and looked at me. "You know what I think, Ryan? I think you should go over there and wish him luck."

"Me?" I said.

"Why not? You were his catcher, weren't you? He's going to be off to some minor league team. If you don't do it soon, you might never get the chance."

It's only about a hundred feet from my house to Josh's, but that was a long walk. I wasn't afraid. I didn't think he was going to punch me out or slam the door in my face. We were past all that. I just wasn't sure what I was doing, or why I was doing it.

When Josh opened his front door and saw me standing there, the huge grin that had been on his face disappeared. He almost looked scared.

"I saw the newspaper article," I said nervously. "I wanted to congratulate you."

He stared at me for a second, as if he had trouble understanding my words. Then his smile returned, broader than ever. "Thanks," he said, his voice bubbling with excitement. "It's great, isn't it? First round. It's what I was hoping for. I didn't even know the Rockies were looking at me. I thought I'd go to the Giants, or maybe the Mariners."

"You don't care though, do you?" I asked.

"Are you kidding! For the money they're going to pay me, I'd play for any team. And it's just the start. It's just the start."

The phone rang inside his house. He looked over his shoulder, then turned back to me. "It's crazy around here. Sports radio stations are calling. Reporters are calling. Lawyers are calling. The Rockies are going to fly me to

Denver for a press conference. Things are happening fast."

"Well, I'll let you go," I said, stepping back and away. "I just wanted to wish you luck."

"Josh!" his father's voice was excited.

"Thanks for coming by," Josh called after me, closing the door. "And good luck to you too, with whatever you end up doing."

Back at my own house, my mother was waiting for me. "How did it go?" she asked.

"I don't know," I said. "Okay, I guess."

My father had about ten projects he wanted me to do that morning, but I didn't have the energy to start any of them. I had a feeling that there was something more important I should be doing, but I couldn't figure out what it was. I ended up going back to my room.

The graduation program was lying on the floor by my bed. I picked it up and paged through it. Under everybody's name they'd listed their accomplishments — the scholarships they'd earned, awards, sports, clubs — stuff like that.

It seemed like exciting things were happening for everybody else. Chris Selin was going to Cal Berkeley. Brandon Ruben was off to Oregon. Monica Roby had a full scholarship to Stanford. And Josh was headed to the major leagues.

I tossed the program onto the floor and lay there feeling sorry for myself. But you can do that for only so long. Finally I went downstairs. "Can I borrow the car?" I asked my mother.

"How long do you want it for?"

"About an hour or so. I've got a couple of things I want to do."

She started to ask what, but then checked herself. "The keys are on the table. But don't be gone more than an hour. I've got a house to show this afternoon."

Shoreline Community College is only about fifteen minutes from my house. I'd driven by it a million times, but that was the first time I ever went onto the campus. It was nicer than I thought it would be. Brick buildings, lots of gardens and pathways. The students looked different than I expected, too. They were older and quieter, more serious.

I found the registrar's office and picked up a summer catalog. I sat down in a chair in the office and paged through it. It didn't take me long to find what I was looking for. I took the catalog back to the main desk.

"Is this a university-level course?" I asked.

She looked at the catalog. "Yes, that one transfers."

"How do I get into it?"

She reached under the counter and pulled out a packet of papers. "Fill out this application form, have your high school send us your transcript, and then bring in a check for tuition. You will need to move quickly, though. Summer session starts in two weeks."

I sat down and filled out the form right there. She looked it over, then smiled. "Good luck to you," she said. "I hope you enjoy your time here at Shoreline."

"I hope so too," I said.

I still had a few minutes before I had to head home, so

I walked around the campus some more. The more I saw of it, the more I liked it. I had to fight to keep my excitement from showing. I didn't want to get caught grinning like some fool high school kid.

In front of the student union building there was a big bulletin board covered with notices announcing everything from jazz concerts to protest rallies. There was a lot going on, way more than I expected. I was about to turn away when something in the upper corner caught my eye. I looked again and saw that it was the schedule for the Shoreline Community College baseball team.

I don't know why that surprised me so much. If I'd ever thought about it, I'd have known they had a team. I'd just never thought about it. But there it was, right in front of me, proof positive. My heart raced then. I thought of what Josh told me when I'd first met him: every team can use a backup catcher who is willing to do the dirty work.

When I got home, my mom was waiting for me at the door, her fingers to her lips. "Shhh," she said, stepping out onto the porch and taking the keys from me. "Your grandfather is asleep on the couch."

I tiptoed past him and went upstairs.

I'd only been gone an hour, but my room looked different to me, wrong somehow. I decided to clean it up, to throw out all the clutter and junk from the school year.

It didn't take long. At the very end I picked the mortarboard from graduation off the floor. I stood there holding it, wondering what to do with it.

Finally I opened the bottom drawer of my dresser and

shoved it inside. As I did, my hand touched something hard. I reached in and pulled out my trophy.

For the first time I looked at it closely. *Most Inspirational Player,* the inscription read. Below those words was my name — *Ryan Ward.*

With my sleeve I polished the trophy a little. And instead of putting it back in the drawer, I placed it on top of the dresser. I put my mortarboard right next to it.

I stepped back and looked at them. They looked good, sitting up there. They belonged out, where people could see them. After all, I'd earned them. And who knows, I may just earn something else someday.